amidst
RUINS
and
REMEMBRANCES

AMY NEWBOLD

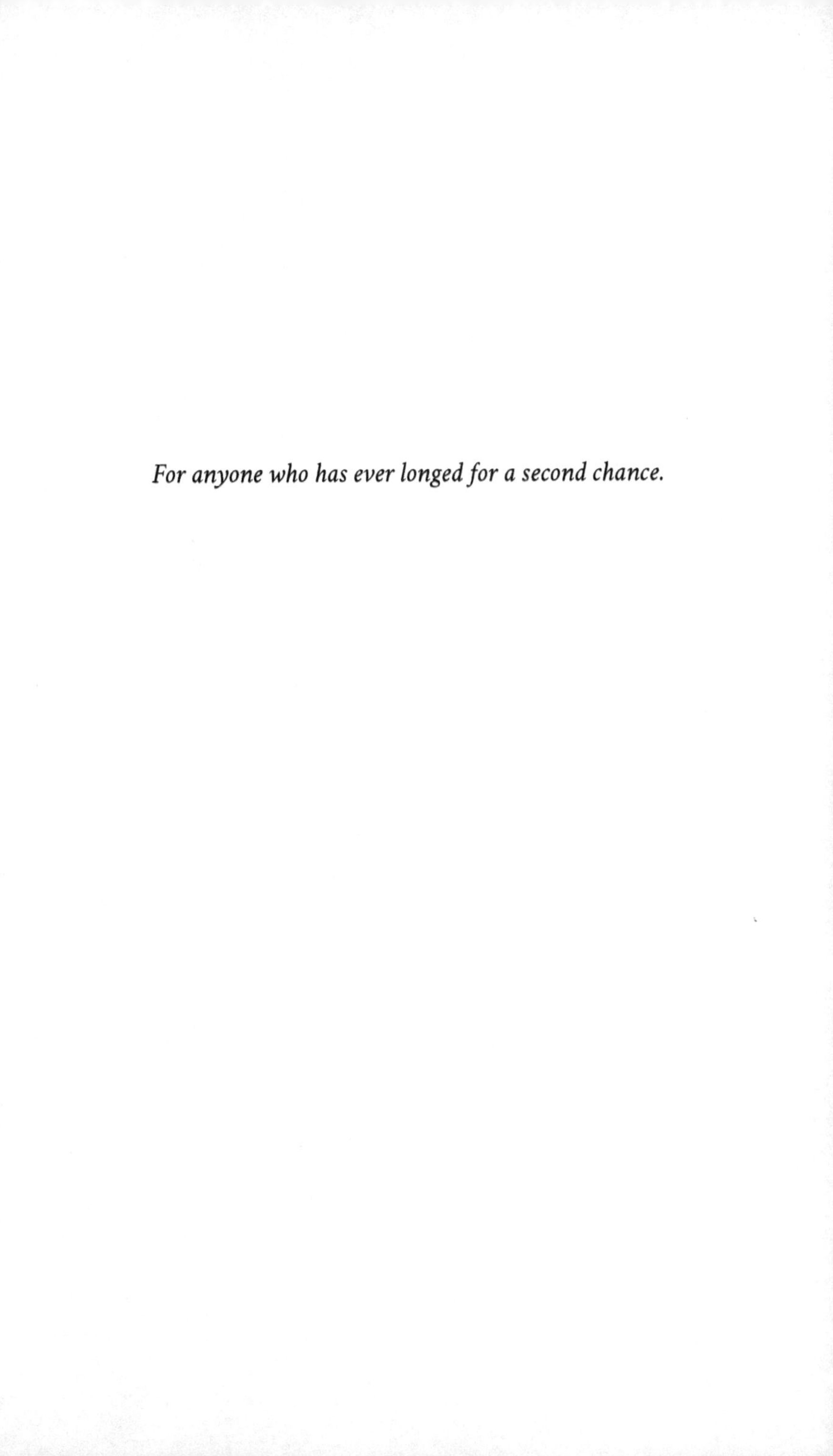

For anyone who has ever longed for a second chance.

CHAPTER 1

Whitby, England 1873

When Eloise Deighton, the only daughter of Matthew and Phoebe Deighton, left Whitby for London to live with her aunt five years ago, she always knew she would return. Whitby, after all, was home to the people that she loved, and the sea that soothed her soul. Living in the city as Aunt Helena's companion had given her opportunities and expanded her horizons, but she'd never gotten completely comfortable with city life. Yet upon her return, everything about Whitby, including her childhood home, was much smaller than she remembered. Now, the very real possibility that she fit neither in the city nor in Whitby loomed large in her mind.

Clad in her chemise, corset, bloomers, and petticoats, she laid a pale green sprigged dress on the bed. It contrasted nicely with the blue dress resting beside it. Both were new, and both represented the lady she had become. She was particularly fond of the blue dress. The cut showed off her waist, and the fabric brought out the color in her eyes. While the dress was in the slimmer style Princess Alexandra wore, without a large bustle or old-fashioned hoop skirts, it was still too fancy for day use in a fishing village. With one last look, she tucked the blue dress away and put on the green one. She fastened the buttons, and turned from side to side, letting the skirt fall over her petticoats and swish about her ankles.

Only last week she had been wearing the grays and purples dictated by mourning customs, but now her time of mourning was officially over. Unfortunately, her heart was not healed from the loss of dear Aunt Helena. They had shared several years of lively companionship before Aunt Helena's health declined. During her final weeks, Helena made Eloise promise she would keep her mourning to the minimum amount of time society required.

Life is for the living, and I insist that you live. Stay here in London, or return to Whitby, but whatever you do, follow your heart, Aunt Helena said. Eloise was determined to do her best to follow that advice. And so, after settling Aunt Helena's affairs, she returned to this seaside town determined to create a life she loved.

Dishes clattered downstairs, reminding Eloise that she should be helping with breakfast. She twisted her hair into a smooth bun and pinned it in place. The mirror reassured her that every strand was exactly where it should be. Satisfied, she went down to the kitchen.

Her very pregnant sister-in-law, Mary, was filling plates for her boys. Two-year-old Thomas took one look at Eloise and, suddenly shy, buried his face in his mother's skirt. Four-year-old Johnny, meanwhile, sat at the table, swinging his legs.

"Let go, Thomas. Why are you clinging so?" Mary glanced over at Eloise. "Good morning. May I get you some food?"

She set the plates on the table and hoisted Thomas onto a chair.

"Why don't you sit down, Mary? I'll get food for both of us." Eloise filled plates with kippers and eggs, hot from the frying pan. She added a few strawberries as a treat before joining Mary at the table. Johnny snatched a strawberry off her plate and popped it in his mouth.

"Mind your manners!" Mary exclaimed.

Johnny responded with an impish grin, juice from the berry dribbling on his chin. Eloise tousled his hair. Neither of the boys remembered her from her few visits to Whitby over the past five years, but Johnny was quickly warming to her presence in the house, and for that she was grateful.

"What are your plans for today?" Mary asked.

"I think I shall start my life as a lady of leisure," Eloise said. Mary laughed. They were childhood friends, and now, since Mary had wed Eloise's older brother, John, they were also family.

"Do you need a companion? I wouldn't mind a day off from all of this," Mary gestured at the boys and the messy kitchen. "Is your inheritance large enough to support us both?"

Eloise smiled. "If only it were. We would travel and see the world."

"That sounds lovely. But my world is here now, with John and the boys. I am rather surprised that you did not find a suitor in London. Surely someone must have captured your attention."

Eloise waved her hand dismissively. "There were so many that it was impossible to choose." Mary laughed again, which was Eloise's intent. What she didn't say was that she had refused the attention of her one and only potential suitor in London because her heart belonged to another; a man she had not seen in ten years.

The stairs creaked as Eloise's father made his way down with his uneven gait. He gripped the railing with one hand and his cane with the other. A smile lit up his weathered face when he saw Eloise. She was not used to seeing him sleep late like this. All of her life, he'd been up at first light getting his fishing boat ready for the day's catch.

"What does a man have to do to get some breakfast around here?" he asked. The twinkle in his eye let Eloise know he was teasing.

It was good to see him happy. Before she'd gone to London, the grief over losing her mother weighed heavily on both of them. The passage of time had brought them much-needed comfort and healing.

Eloise rose from her chair. "Sit, Father. I'll get you something."

"Thank you. It is good to have you home." He studied her for a moment. "You look just like your mother."

Her cheeks flushed at the compliment. Mother was the prettiest woman she'd ever known and had an elegance and refinement about her that Eloise tried hard to emulate. She filled a plate and set it before him.

"Thank you," he said, his eyes wistful. Eloise knew he would rather be out in the coble with John than here at home with the women and children. Since his leg injury last fall, he'd had to leave the fishing business to his son.

"Are you going to walk on the promenade with the rich folks in your fancy London clothes today?" Father asked.

Only the wealthiest residents of Whitby joined the rich tourists in walking the promenade to socialize. Eloise was flattered that he thought she was worthy of joining them. While it was tempting to show off her city manners and finery, part of her still doubted that she would fit in.

"I am helping Mary today. The promenade will have to wait," Eloise said, keeping her tone light.

"I met your mother on the promenade," Father said. "It was an unusually cold day, and a storm swept in. I offered her my coat as protection from the rain. She accepted, and somehow managed to find me later to return it. I'm still surprised she chose to leave her city life behind to marry a fisherman."

Eloise never grew tired of hearing the story of her parents. It was because of their example that she was certain she would only marry if she could have a love like theirs. Her heart had been broken once, and she was determined to protect it from being hurt again.

"You should go to the promenade," Father said. "You are as fine as any other woman there. And you never know—perhaps you'll meet a gentleman that you'll fancy. It's not too late for you to make a good match."

Eloise loved that he did not think of her as past her prime now that she was the ripe old age of twenty-seven. But she had not come back here to hunt for a husband. She had returned to find her own place in the world. A room to rent. Good books and good friends to pass the time.

"I don't need to find a husband on the promenade, Father, especially not one from out of town. I am perfectly content to stay here in Whitby without one."

Father reached in his pocket and pulled out a brown, curved stone. He set it on the table and pushed it toward her. "Found this on the beach the day I got your letter saying you were coming home. I thought you might like to have it. Do you still like fossils, or have you outgrown them?"

Eloise picked up the small, fossilized ammonite. She traced the ridges of the creature with her finger.

"Thank you for remembering," she said. "I do still love these."

The fossil was smaller than the one she had tucked away in her trunk upstairs. Ten years ago, she'd run off to a rocky beach with the young man who'd stolen her heart. Together they'd found a smooth, rounded rock. When they split it open, it revealed two ammonite fossils inside. He kept one half, and she kept the other, promising that they would reunite the two halves when he returned. It was to be the beginning of their life together.

But he hadn't come back, and she had learned over the years that it was best to let the past remain in the past. They'd been so young. He was nineteen and she was only seventeen. Still, she could not stop the images of Griffith Hastings that flooded her mind. His wavy brown hair. His brilliant smile.

She shook off the memory and kissed her father on the cheek. "Thank you. I'll take this to my room and then I'll clean up the dishes."

CHAPTER 2

Griffith Hastings drank in the familiar landscape from the train window as they drew nearer to Whitby. The last time he'd traveled to this seaside town, Father was with him, and his younger brother, Robert. Griffith had loved coming to Whitby during the summer months. Then Father died, and he hadn't been back all these years. Now Robert was married and had stayed behind in London to run the business while Griffith was away.

Memories flooded his mind: the cries of the shorebirds, the warmth of the sand, the rhythm of the waves, the salty scent in the air. He couldn't wait to buy ices from the stand to share with his daughter, Victoria. He'd take her up the endless steps to the abbey ruins. Perhaps he'd even teach her to swim.

Victoria, lulled by the motion of the train, dozed in her seat, leaning on his mother, a doll clutched in her arms. Her hair, dark brown like his own, hung in ringlets to her shoulders. Her skin was pale in contrast to the plum-colored dress she wore. The ruffled skirt hung just below her knees, and her black-booted feet did not reach the floor.

Mother sat as still as the motion of the train allowed. Even after a morning of travel, her hat was in place and her dress was unwrinkled. Only her hands, twisting her handkerchief, revealed her tension. She was careful not to disturb the sleeping child even as she crumpled the piece of fabric.

"We're almost there," Griffith said to reassure her.

She gave him a weak smile. "I hope you know what you are doing."

He did not respond. While he couldn't wait to return to Whitby, his mother was not so eager, and nothing he said would change that. She had reluctantly agreed to come on the trip to help him with Victoria, and he was grateful. It was his hope that spending a few weeks by the sea would be healing for both him and his daughter.

Griffith reached in his pocket and fingered the small, white shell he carried. It was part of a secret code he'd created with the girl he once knew. They found a hidden hollow in the low sea wall near the sweet shop. Placing a shell in the hollow signaled that they would meet on the beach for a morning swim. Whoever found the shell switched it with a different one to confirm the meeting. He smiled at the memory.

"I have reserved rooms for us at the Carriage Inn," Mother said. "It should be most comfortable."

Griffith frowned. "What about the Seaside Inn where we used to stay?"

"That old place? We are well-enough off now to stay someplace nicer, Griffith. It will be better for Victoria. Not so close to the water, or the piers. We must keep an eye on her."

He sighed and hoped that their time by the shore would not be stifled by the overprotectiveness of his mother. He had roamed free in Whitby for four summers, from the time he was fifteen. But Victoria was only six, far too young to wander on her own.

Victoria shifted in her sleep, and Mother soothed her. He didn't know what he would have done without his mother's help after his wife, Rebecca, died two years ago. While Victoria had only been four years old, he knew she missed her mother terribly.

The train pulled into the station, and he scooped up Victoria. "Wake up, little one. We are here."

Victoria rubbed her eyes and blinked in the bright light of day. "Where is the sea, Papa?"

"You will see it soon enough. We must get our trunks and arrange a ride to the inn. Once we are settled in our rooms, I shall take you to see the water."

Mother cleared her throat. "I believe we will need some food before you take her sightseeing. We are here for weeks, Griffith. What is the rush?"

Griffith inhaled deeply. The smell of the sea combined with the pungent scent of the fish market in a familiar way that welcomed him back. It was just as he remembered. Beside him, Mother wrinkled her nose.

"I shall never get used to the smell of fish," she said, raising her handkerchief to her face. "It is one of the things I dislike about the shore."

Victoria wrinkled her nose in imitation of her grandmother, making Griffith wish they had made the trip alone. He retrieved their luggage and found a hackney to take them to the inn. Once their trunks were loaded, Griffith helped Mother and Victoria take their seats. As they drove, he pointed out the places he remembered to Victoria. She was wide-eyed, taking everything in, but she stayed silent.

Victoria was often quiet now that her mother was gone. Griffith hoped time in Whitby would change that, would bring some color to her cheeks, bring back the smile on her face. And the chatter. He missed her chatter.

When they arrived at the inn, Mother entered the building to confirm their rooms were ready. She returned a moment later, fuming.

"They have rented all the rooms and say there is not anywhere for us to stay. You must fix this, Griffith. And don't take no for an answer."

"I'll handle it," Griffith said, annoyed that she doubted his ability to do so. He may have needed her during his grief, but he was not a child. He was perfectly capable of securing lodgings.

Griffith went inside and spoke with the innkeeper, who was apologetic. There was no help for it. All of the rooms at the Carriage Inn were indeed occupied. The man suggested some other places, including the Seaside Inn where they used to stay. Mother would not be happy, but Griffith's heart picked up its pace. It was exactly as he'd wanted it, as if Fate were intervening on his behalf. He hurried back outside.

"We are going to have to stay at the Seaside Inn, I'm afraid," he said to Mother. "Come, Victoria. Let's stretch our legs. Mother, why don't you ride ahead with our luggage?"

"You did not do as I asked. You should have insisted on our rooms." Mother huffed in frustration.

"It will be fine, you'll see," Griffith said. He gave the driver the new location. As the hackney pulled away, he grasped Victoria's hand. She walked placidly beside him.

"Are you hungry?" he asked.

She nodded. He stopped at a stand and purchased fish and chips. Mother would balk at the street food, saying it was uncouth and inappropriate for someone of their standing. Griffith, however, hoped it would taste as good as he remembered. The vendor sprinkled vinegar on the hot, battered fish, and Griffith's mouth watered in anticipation.

Victoria blew on her portion before taking a small bite. She chewed carefully, as if she were trying to decide what she thought of it.

He was rewarded when her face lit up. The food was good, no matter what Mother's opinion of it was. He thought it was the perfect quick meal after a morning of travel. Griffith led Victoria to a nearby bench, and they sat down to eat.

"Will Grandmama be worried about us?"

"She knows I can find my way around. I used to come here every summer," he said.

"What did you do?"

He tipped his head back, letting the sun warm his face as memories flooded his mind. Sneaking out for morning swims, finding fossils, stealing kisses.

"I swam almost every day, ate boiled sweets, and climbed the steps to the abbey. We shall do all of those things while we are here," he said.

Victoria's eyes were wide, and her voice was small. "Do girls swim?"

He knew one girl who swam. Better than he did, even in the heavy dress and bloomers women had to wear. Brushing memories of her aside, he answered Victoria's question. "Queen Victoria enjoys swimming, and as her namesake, I think you might try it this summer. If it is all right for the queen, I am sure it is all right for you. What do you think?"

He could almost see the information turning over and over in her mind. "Maybe I'll swim. But what if the water scares me?"

"Then we shall walk along the shore and let the waves kiss your toes. You don't have to swim to enjoy the beach." They finished eating and he rose from the bench, reaching for Victoria's hand. "Grandmama will be waiting for us. We'd best get to the inn."

The Seaside Inn had not changed. From the gray stone

walls and the red-tiled roof to the weathered sign in need of a fresh coat of paint—all of it was as he remembered. He could not suppress a grin as he led Victoria through the door.

"Welcome home," he said.

Mother was nowhere in sight, but some of their trunks waited near the counter. Tables and chairs filled the common room where they would take their meals. Victoria squeezed his hand.

"Where's Grandmama?"

"She is getting your room all set up for you," he said.

"Will I be with you?"

"No, you and Grandmama will be sharing a room, but I shall be close by. You will be quite comfortable here."

He hoped she would be. He hoped she would love Whitby as much as he did. If all went well, he'd be tempted to stay here and not return to London.

Once in his room, he quickly arranged his belongings. He placed the little white shell on top of the dresser, and alongside it, he put a fossil the size of his hand. It had come from this place, and while he only had half of it, he knew who had the other half. It was too much to hope that the halves would be reunited during this trip, but he could not deny that he wanted the opportunity.

Eloise Deighton was unlike any girl he'd ever known. Long, brown hair, often worn loose, hanging down past her shoulders. Moody eyes changing like the sea. Bare feet, lightly tanned skin. Lilting laughter like musical notes. And lips so soft he never wanted to stop kissing them.

He wondered if she was in Whitby still. If she were living here, she was probably married. With children. He ran his finger over the curved shape of the ammonites in the rock… one raised, one indented. Had she kept her half?

He'd loved Eloise and had abandoned her. He'd loved his

wife, Rebecca, and she had died. Absently, his hand rose to the scar on his cheek. Sorrow seemed to follow him everywhere. Except here. He'd been happy in Whitby, and he longed to be happy here once again.

Even if Eloise were not married, even if he apologized for the way things ended between them, it was hard for him to imagine her wanting to see him again. Too much water was under the bridge. His focus needed to be on Victoria and her happiness. It was for the best.

CHAPTER 3

The next afternoon, Eloise hurried down the cobblestone street toward the beach. The stone and brick houses gave way to a row of shops, several selling Whitby jet jewelry. Ever since Queen Victoria wore a piece made from the black gemstone to Prince Albert's funeral, the jewelry had soared in popularity, and now there were more craftsmen here than ever before.

When Eloise reached the promenade, it was already crowded with tourists. She was not there to mingle, however, but had an errand to complete. Mary wanted an ice, and she'd requested one from the cart near the bandstand. That vendor, Mary insisted, had the very best flavors and portions.

A loud cry drew her attention. As she came nearer, she saw two young ladies had collided and tumbled to the ground. One sprang to her feet and berated the other, her voice shrill.

"How dare you? You barged through the crowd as if you are of some importance, which obviously you are not."

Noticing a smudge of dirt on her dress, she turned to the woman beside her. "Mother, look what she has done!"

The mother and daughter were clearly tourists with their fine dresses, hats, and gloves. The mother bent to retrieve a dropped parasol and handed it to her daughter.

Meanwhile, the girl on the ground cowered as people stopped to watch the spectacle. Eloise's heart went out to her. She had been that girl, wearing a plain dress and having flushed cheeks and disheveled hair. She knew the humiliation of being out of place in all this finery. Eloise made her way to the girl's side and helped her to her feet.

"Are you hurt?" she asked.

The girl shook her head, and in a voice barely above a whisper, said, "It was an accident."

Eloise faced the mother and daughter. "She did not mean to. Surely you can see that."

The mother glared at Eloise, who held her ground. Aunt Helena always told her to keep her head high and walk tall. *People will think you belong.* She squared her shoulders and met the woman's gaze.

"She should be more careful," the woman said, and steered her daughter away from the crowd of spectators.

"Thank you." The girl's voice was timid.

Eloise smiled at her. "You have every right to be here. Don't you forget that."

The girl nodded and slipped away.

Eloise found the cart near the bandstand and ordered ice cream. "It's for Mary Deighton," she said. "Is it all right if I return the glass later?"

"For Mary? Of course," the vendor said. He heaped the frozen treat over the brim of the glass and handed it to Eloise. As she carried the treat back home, a drip slid over the edge and ran onto her gloved hand. If she didn't deliver it soon, it would be nothing but a creamy puddle in the little container. But hurrying was impossible with so many people out strolling today.

The ice continued to drip down her glove, leaving a sticky trail over her hand and wrist. Eloise walked faster, hoping to reach Mary while the treat was still cold. In her hurry, she nearly tripped over a child.

The girl was crying, tears rolling down her cheeks and spilling onto her white dress. A red bow adorned her dark brown hair. Eloise glanced around but couldn't identify any adults who might be with the girl. If she stopped to help, she would have to discard the ice and disappoint Mary. But she couldn't leave the little one alone like this in the crowd.

Ignoring the people jostling around her, she knelt beside the girl. "Are you lost?"

"I can't find my father," the girl said, her lip trembling.

"What's your name?"

"Victoria."

"That's a fine name, just like the queen. My name is Eloise. Shall we move over there out of this crowd?"

The girl took her free hand, and the gesture tugged at Eloise's heart. The child was so trusting. They made their way to the edge of the promenade.

"Would you like this?" she said, offering Victoria the melting ice.

Victoria accepted the treat, her tear-stained cheeks rosy in the sun. Eloise rummaged through her bag and pulled out a handkerchief. She gently wiped the girl's tears.

"Where did you last see your father?"

Victoria licked the ice cream before answering. "He stopped to talk to someone, and now I can't see him. Do you think he went on without me?"

"Of course not. See how many people there are? He's lost sight of you, that's all. I am sure he is looking for you right now, and if we stay in one place, he will find us."

"Will you wait with me?" Victoria asked.

"Yes, I'll stay until he finds you."

While many people were walking on the promenade, several more sat on the benches lining the path, people-watching. Eloise was fortunate to spot an unoccupied bench, and she helped Victoria stand on it. "It'll be easier for him to see you now."

Victoria placed her hand on Eloise's arm to steady herself.

"Now, tell me what your father looks like. Do you remember what he was wearing today?"

Victoria furrowed her brow. Eloise noticed her eyes were a startling shade of green. A shade she had only ever seen in one other person. It had to be a coincidence, though. She'd accepted the fact that Griffith would never return to Whitby.

"He is wearing a hat," Victoria said. "And he is tall."

Getting a useful description from the child proved to be impossible. Eloise scanned the crowd, watching for a tall man who had lost something very precious.

"What if he doesn't find me?"

"He will," Eloise said. "Do you live here in Whitby?"

"I'm from London," Victoria said.

"Do you know the name of the place where you are staying?"

"The Seaside Inn."

"If we don't find your father, I'll take you to the inn. I know it well." Mary's parents ran the place, and Griffith used to stay there. But she mustn't let memories of Griffith distract her now. The girl was all that mattered. "I am sure he will come for you very soon," Eloise said, although she wasn't sure at all. But she didn't want Victoria to start crying again. The world should be a safe place for children.

The afternoon sun was unusually warm, and Eloise longed for an ice herself. She adjusted her hat and tucked a stray strand of hair behind her ear. Today was not going at all how she had planned.

But Mary would understand. She would want Eloise to help Victoria.

"My Grandmama was with me too," Victoria said.

How could two adults have lost her? Eloise sighed. Children moved so quickly when you weren't watching. Maybe Victoria would remember something else that would be helpful, like where she had been when she'd last seen them. "Did you stop to look at something? In a shop window, maybe?"

"I wanted to see the horses," Victoria said, taking another lick of the ice cream.

"By the bathing machines?"

Victoria nodded and pointed to the row of carts lined up on the beach. Several had been pulled by horses into the water, and women were bathing in the shallows with attendants on hand to pull them out if needed. Eloise didn't consider sliding into knee-high water from a bathing machine to be real swimming, but it was the only socially acceptable way for women to swim.

"Do you like horses?" Eloise asked, hoping to distract the girl from her predicament.

"Yes. Do you think they like pulling carts into the water?"

Eloise had never really considered it. "They don't seem to be putting up a fuss, so I imagine they don't mind," she said. "Do you see your father anywhere?"

Victoria rose up on her toes, tightening her grip on Eloise's arm. "Not yet."

"He'll come," Eloise said, hoping she was right.

CHAPTER 4

Griffith came to an abrupt stop on the promenade causing several people to bump into him. He ignored their protests and spun in a circle, scanning the crowd for Victoria. She had to be here somewhere. She'd been by his side when an acquaintance stopped to speak to him. He'd let go of her hand for a moment, only a moment. Now she was gone.

He moved to the edge of the walkway, fighting the panic rising in his throat. If anything happened to her, he would not be able to bear it. Nowhere in the swarm of people did he see Victoria's red hair bow or white dress.

He shouted her name, hoping she would hear him. The adrenaline surging through his body spurred him to action. He pressed through the crowd, nudging people aside as he went.

"Victoria!"

No white dress. No red ribbon. No answer to his shouts.

He noted the name of a shop as he passed it. He had to keep track of where he had searched. Would she have wandered this far? He determined to go no further until he retraced his steps. As he headed back the way he had come, the current of people made progress difficult.

He called for her again.

Please let her be safe. It was almost, but not quite, a prayer. He hadn't prayed much since losing his wife, but he might start again now.

He spotted his mother coming out of a bakery, parcel in hand. When he reached her, he gripped her elbow. "Is Victoria with you?"

A flash of worry crossed her face. "No. I left her with you, Griffith."

He groaned. "She is lost. I can't find her."

Mother dropped her package in alarm. She glanced up and down the promenade. "How long has she been gone?"

Sweat beaded on his upper lip. He should never have brought her to the promenade when it was this crowded. He should have taken her to the beach instead or stayed at the inn with her and read her a story. Where could she be?

"We'll find her, Griffith. She can't have gone far," Mother said.

Griffith retrieved the package and placed it in his mother's trembling hands. "I'll continue this way. Why don't you head in that direction?"

Mother agreed, and they separated. As he wound through the crowd, Griffith called Victoria's name at regular intervals. He checked each storefront to see if a display had attracted her attention. It was out of character for her to venture forth on her own. She wasn't particularly brave.

When he reached the end of the promenade with no sign of Victoria, despair caused the panic in him to boil over. He covered his face with his hands, fighting the tears burning his eyes. He wanted to shout at the universe. He wanted to shake his fist at the blue sky and demand fairness from the powers that be. But such demands, he knew from sad experience, were futile. None of his prayers or wishes saved his wife, and he couldn't trust them to bring Victoria back to him now. He must find her on his own.

Griffith wiped his face with his handkerchief and walked with the crowd. This time he moved more methodically. When he saw people seated on a bench or stopped in conversation, he approached them.

"Have you seen a little girl? I'm trying to find my daughter. She's wearing a white dress." He gestured with his hands, showing her height. They all expressed concern and all shook their heads. He told them where he was staying in case they found her and then continued on.

Music wafted through the air as the band began playing. Perhaps the sound had drawn her attention. When he reached the bandstand, he wove through the spectators gathered on the lawn. No white dress or red hair ribbon anywhere. As he continued to search, every minute was agony.

With a ragged sigh, he headed back to find his mother. He clung to the hope that Mother had found her. Victoria wouldn't have gone to the water, would she? Been washed out to sea by a rogue wave?

As he peered at the water, the sea was calm. Gentle waves rolled onto the shore. Even if she had ventured out on the beach, it was unlikely that she had been washed away. In the distance, he saw the bathing machines lined up on the sand. She liked horses. He would check there next, after he found his mother.

And then he saw her, standing on a bench, the bright sunlight reflecting off her white dress. He raced toward her.

"Victoria!"

"Papa!"

He scooped her up in his arms and hugged her tight. She nestled her head against his shoulder.

"I couldn't find you," she said. She lifted her head and cupped his cheeks in her small hands. "I was scared."

"I was frightened, too. I'm sorry I lost you." His heart raced and he took a deep breath to calm it.

"Eloise helped me," Victoria said, gesturing at the woman standing beside the bench.

His Eloise? Could it be?

He tightened his grip on Victoria as he peered past her. The woman met his gaze, and his heart leapt. Her eyes were like the sea, clear blue one moment like a summer sky, gray the next like the sea during a storm. Her brown hair was coiled and pinned beneath a hat instead of hanging down her back, and she was wearing stylish shoes, no longer barefoot. But despite all the changes to her appearance, he would know her anywhere.

"Eloise." His voice cracked.

Her face was pale beneath her hat, as if she had seen a ghost. Her expression was hard to describe. Not surprise, exactly. More like shock. Her voice was so quiet he could hardly hear her. "Griffith."

"Are you…is it still…Miss Deighton?"

She drew a slow, steady breath and a hint of color returned to her cheeks. "I have not yet married." She set her jaw, her gaze challenging him. "I never thought I would see you again after all this time.

Griffith searched her face. In her eyes, he saw only distance and a whisper of pain. "It has been a long time, I'm afraid. Too long," he said. "I can never thank you enough for finding Victoria and for coming to her aid."

Eloise smoothed her gloves. "I'm happy to be of help. Victoria is delightful. And very brave."

Victoria, her face smudged with chocolate ice, patted Griffith's shoulder. "She said if we waited here for you that you would find us."

"She was right. We are very fortunate," Griffith said, smoothing his daughter's hair.

Eloise took a step away from him. "All's well that ends well. I have to get home. Please excuse me."

He placed a hand on her arm. "Don't go. There are things to say."

She shifted, moving her arm from beneath his touch. Her eyes lingered on his cheek, the one with the scar. "Years ago, there were things to say, but all of that is washed away and it is too late. You have your life, Mr. Hastings, and I have mine." With that, she disappeared into the crowd.

Griffith's jaw tightened when she called him Mr. Hastings, and the muscle on his cheek twitched beneath the scar. Was her hurried departure more than the shock of seeing him again? He was not the same man she had known. He bore scars not only on his face, but also on his heart. He fought the temptation to go after her.

"Put me down, Papa." Victoria wriggled in his arms.

She was growing heavy. "You must stay right beside me." He set her on her feet. Going after Eloise would have to wait.

"Don't let go." Victoria squeezed his fingers.

"Never," he said. "Your hand is sticky. I don't think I could let go if I wanted to."

"Eloise gave me an ice."

"That was very kind of Miss Deighton. Come, let's go find Grandmama and let her know you are safe and sound."

He glanced once over his shoulder, knowing that he would not be able to see Eloise. But that didn't stop him from trying.

Eloise Deighton was unmarried, still living here in Whitby. Now that the panic over losing Victoria was subsiding, he was keenly aware of a new sensation rising within him. Something he had not experienced for a long time. Hope. Seeing Eloise made him realize she still held a piece of his heart.

CHAPTER 5

$\mathcal{E}$loise didn't return home immediately. She wouldn't be able to hide from Mary that something had happened, and she wasn't ready to talk about Griffith yet. She passed the fish market and headed down the East Pier. It was, thankfully, not busy at this time of day, the fishermen having returned already with their morning catch. She walked to the end and gazed out over the water as she had done so many times before.

Griffith Hastings was back in Whitby. Not only was he back, but he had a daughter. Which implied he also had a wife.

She shouldn't have been surprised that he had moved on. It made sense, but that didn't stop a thick lump from forming in her throat. Somehow the idea of him having a family was less painful when he was far away. Seeing him and having to confront the reality of his circumstances was a different matter. Her hands trembled and she clasped them together to still them.

Gulls called as the waves gently washed under the pier. She closed her eyes, letting the sound of the water soothe her. If the promenade and public beach weren't so crowded, she'd go to the private cove where she used to swim. But she couldn't face winding back through the crowd, nor did she want to risk seeing him again.

How dare he? How dare he come back with his child in tow as if nothing had happened? He spoke to her without one ounce of regret. No apologies. He was not the person she remembered. The person she had loved. He had walked away from her so easily after making promises to her. Perhaps he had never been who she thought he was.

When her nerves were sufficiently calmed, she walked home. Her father was nowhere in sight, and Thomas was napping. Mary did not look up from the book she was reading to Johnny.

Eloise slipped upstairs and removed her sticky glove, rinsing it in the basin.

Work will take away the sting. Aunt Helena's wisdom had gotten her through her worst times. They often worked in the small garden behind the London house or did needlework to keep their hands busy. Now Eloise went to the kitchen, determined to keep herself occupied.

She wiped the counter and swept the floor. Next, she tackled the shelves. She removed plates, cups, and bowls, and washed each shelf, drying it thoroughly before returning the dishes.

"You are full of energy." Mary stood in the doorway.

"Yes."

"Was the vendor out of ice?"

Eloise stopped cleaning. "I'm sorry, Mary. I stumbled across a lost little girl, and I ended up giving the ice to her."

Mary found a cloth and scrubbed the counter. "At least someone enjoyed it. Did you find her parents?"

Eloise nodded. "Her father."

"A happy ending, then."

Eloise straightened the plates on the now-clean shelf. "I suppose."

Mary paused in her cleaning. "What's wrong?"

Her shoulders slumped and she perched on the stool. She might as well tell Mary. Perhaps Mary had some wisdom to offer her.

"It was Griffith. He is the girl's father."

Mary leaned against the counter. "He's back?"

Eloise nodded, miserable. "I must admit it was very unexpected, seeing him again."

"Yes, I can imagine," Mary said. "Does he look the same?"

"Yes, and no. He has broader shoulders and a scar on his cheek. But he is still handsome. And his eyes...." Eloise fingered the counter, tracing a groove in the wood with her thumbnail. "Mary, what will I do? I don't want to run into him all over town."

"If you run into him, you will be polite. But hopefully you won't have to see him. Did you meet his wife?"

"She wasn't there. Only Griffith and his daughter. She has his eyes."

Mary said nothing, and for that, Eloise was grateful. It was one of the things she appreciated most about her friend —her ability to be supportive without telling Eloise how to think or feel. Thomas wandered in, sucking on two of his fingers. His hair was mussed, and his face was lined with sleep. Eloise reached for him and to her surprise, Thomas came to her. He was a welcome distraction from Griffith and her tangle of feelings.

"Why don't you rest, Mary? I'll keep him entertained and then I'll make something for dinner."

As Mary left the kitchen, she squeezed Eloise's shoulder. "Everything will work out as it is meant to," she said.

Eloise wished she could believe her.

WHEN SUPPER WAS FINISHED and the dishes done, Eloise escaped out the front door and hurried down the promenade. The sun wouldn't set until later, and tourists were taking advantage of the cooler evening air as they strolled along the walkway.

The bathing machines rested in a tidy row away from the water, the horses having been taken away for the night. The beach was empty. Eloise stepped onto the sand and walked toward the rocks that barred the end of the beach. When she reached them, she glanced around to make sure no one was watching before clambering over the rocks and making her way into the next cove.

The crumbling cliffs welcomed her. She sank down on a large boulder nestled in the sand. At last, she let her afternoon encounter with Griffith wash over her like a wave breaking on the shore. Tears streamed down her cheeks. She thought she had put any feelings for Griffith Hastings behind her but seeing him proved that was not true.

The breeze off the water cooled her flushed cheeks. This place was her refuge. Griffith disrupted that when he started coming here, but then it became the place she shared with him. Little had changed in the years she'd been away.

She remembered him the way he'd been when she first met him fifteen years ago. He was scrawny, shy, and not as strong a swimmer as she was. That first morning, he hadn't been wearing a stitch of clothing, never dreaming that a girl would be in the water. Her lips twitched into a smile at the memory. He was embarrassed, and insisted she get out of the water first.

It was the beginning of a fragile friendship, for she refused to give up her morning swims, and he, now wearing clothing, joined her. Each summer he returned to Whitby, and each summer their friendship grew.

Eloise lay back on the rock. It was still warm from the afternoon heat. She closed her eyes, letting the rhythm of the waves wash through her memories until her favorite one rose to the surface. She'd been seventeen that summer…

THE SEA WAS calm that morning when she had gone for her morning swim. The swells lifted her gently as she floated on her back, waiting for Griffith. His family was overdue that summer, and she was anxious for his return.

"Boo."

His voice startled her, and she took in a mouthful of water. Sputtering and coughing, she fought to clear her lungs.

"I should think you would be better at swimming after all these years," Griffith teased.

"You made me choke!" Despite pretending to be angry, she couldn't help smiling at him.

"Rest against me until you catch your breath." He moved behind her, steadying her with an arm around her waist. His closeness, his ease with her surprised her. Each summer, they'd had to learn to be together again, to settle into a rhythm. But not this time. This time, it was as if they had never been apart.

She leaned back against his chest, absorbing his strength. His body was warm against hers in the morning chill. Familiar, yet new. She coughed again and then drew a deep breath, inhaling and exhaling slowly, not wanting to move.

"All right?" he asked.

She was more than all right now that he had returned.

When Griffith was here, she could breathe again. Be herself. He always made her feel like she belonged.

"Yes," she said. He rested his cheek against her hair with an intimacy that had not been between them before.

She turned to face him, and he encircled her waist with his arms, pulling her close. His jaw was chiseled, the soft cheeks of a boy giving way to the leaner face of a man. Traces of fine hair were visible on his chest through his wet shirt. She placed her hands on his shoulders, not knowing where else to put them.

His green eyes caught and held her gaze. Gingerly, she reached out and traced the stubble on his face. He was no longer a child, and neither was she. His eyes bored into her soul with an intensity that startled her.

If she swam away now, things between them might remain unchanged. It was a moment on the brink, on the cusp of something new. If she stayed, nothing between them would ever be the same.

"Eloise," he said, his voice hoarse.

He traced her lips with his finger, and she trembled. *We shouldn't be here, she thought. We should not be starting off the summer this way, so close. On the verge of a....*

She closed her eyes, waiting for the press of his lips against hers, longing for her first kiss.

"Griff! There you are!" A male voice shattered the moment.

Eloise pulled away from Griffith as the intruder swam toward them, his head bobbing in the waves. Griffith positioned himself between her and the boy.

"What are you doing here, Robert?" he called, all tenderness gone from his voice.

Griffith's brother. She'd never met him. They had always managed to sneak off without Robert following them, until now. How could Fate be so cruel? She was certain Griffith was about to kiss her.

"I came to swim with you," Robert said.

"I'll race you to the shore," Griffith said, and she knew he was protecting her from being discovered out on this forbidden swim.

"I just got here," the boy protested. "Who is that with you? Can't we all swim together?"

Eloise took a breath and plunged under the water. Pulling hard, she swam toward some nearby rocks. The waves were choppy as she surfaced, and she fought her way through them.

Griffith and the boy were still conversing. The boy kept turning his head this way and that, looking for her.

Clinging to the craggy surface of the rocks, Eloise absorbed the force of the waves the best she could. One large wave hit her in the head, slamming her face into the rough surface. At last, she managed to pull herself up on the rocks, scraping her knees and feet. She could still see Griffith but could not hear what he was saying. He looked toward her, and she lifted her hand to signal that she was all right. He raised his arm in return and swam toward the shore.

The crisis of being discovered together was averted. Eloise leaned back against the rocks and swiped her hand across her forehead. It came away streaked with blood. She pressed the hem of her swim dress against the cut to stem the flow. Griffith Hastings had almost kissed her. He was back for the summer, and she didn't know when, but she was willing to bet he would try again. And she wanted him to.

ELOISE SHOOK off the memory and rose to her feet. That day with Griffith had been filled with possibilities. Over the summer, their friendship had evolved into something more. They'd swum together many times, shared ices, climbed to the abbey ruins, and more. When he left, he promised that when he came back, they'd let their families know of their intentions to be together. All winter she had waited, eager to be with him.

That was ten years ago. The next summer, he hadn't come back. She'd never gotten an explanation as to why he didn't return. She watched for him during many lonely mornings at the beach. When she finally summoned her courage and wrote to him, her letters went unanswered. At first, she'd been hurt. And then angry. As the summer stretched on without him, Eloise had stopped swimming.

Now, after all this time, she wasn't sure what her feelings were. He was back, but it was too late. Maybe it was good, though, that she had not only seen Griffith, but also talked to him. She'd survived. While seeing him had shaken her, she was happy to note that her heart was mostly intact. The worst was over. Now that he had returned, the memories would no longer haunt her. She only had to weather the storm of these few weeks and then he would go back to London, and she would be free of him forever. Until he left, she would do her best to avoid him.

But despite her resolve, as she walked home, she remembered the little things he did. The way he hummed when he swam alongside her, the way he always had her choose her favorite kind of boiled sweet. How often had he surprised her with an unusual seashell? She missed his arms around her as they watched the first stars appearing after dusk. For years, she thought she no longer had feelings for Griffith, but now, she was no longer sure.

CHAPTER 6

Griffith stood before the red brick home and doffed his hat, running his hand over the brim while he gathered his courage. He rapped on the door and waited. Heavy footsteps sounded inside the house, and he took a step back, stealing himself to meet the occupant. Many times, he had thought about what he would say to Eloise when he got the chance, but now that he stood on her doorstep, all of his plans flew from his head. He feared he would make a mess of it.

The door opened and a man with a weathered face greeted him. His beard was graying, as was his thinning hair, and he leaned on a cane. But it was his eyes that caught Griffith's attention. Eloise had the same eyes. This man must be her father.

Griffith cleared his throat. "I've come to see Miss Eloise Deighton. Is she in?"

The man eyed him up and down. "What do you want with her?"

"My daughter was separated from me on the promenade

yesterday. Miss Deighton found Victoria and took care of her until we could be reunited. I did not get the chance to adequately express my gratitude to her, and I've come to do so now."

"Daughter, eh? And where is your wife?"

"I'm widowed, sir," Griffith said. He had hoped that Eloise would invite him in, maybe even offer him some tea. Or, even better, he'd imagined the two of them walking down to the beach as they used to do. Maybe they could steal a moment of privacy. He had not anticipated being questioned by her father.

"I haven't seen you around town. You don't live here, do you?"

"No, sir. I'm from London. My family used to come to Whitby every summer, although it has been some time since I have been back."

At that, the man cast a sharp glare at him, his eyes piercing. "How long?"

"Pardon?" Griffith asked, confused by the man's question.

"How long has it been since you've come to Whitby?"

Griffith's mouth was suddenly dry. He cleared his throat. "It has been about ten years, Mr. Deighton."

He took a chance assuming that the man was Eloise's father. They had not been properly introduced. But the man did not correct him.

"Ten years since you were here. And you saw Eloise today, but not for the first time, I imagine." Mr. Deighton made no move to open the door wider or to invite Griffith inside. Nor did he give any indication that he would call Eloise to the door.

This had been a mistake, coming here. What did he think he would accomplish? Of course, Eloise would not want to see him again. Meeting Victoria and learning Griffith had a family had to have been a blow. He wondered how much Mr.

Deighton knew. Had Eloise come home upset after their encounter today? Had she told him about their shared history? Although he may never be able to set things right with Eloise, he had to try.

"I would like to see Miss Deighton if I may. Even if it is only for a moment."

The man grunted and swung the door open. "She is not here, but come in."

Griffith had no desire to go inside if Eloise wasn't home. "I don't want to trouble you. If you tell me when I might find her here, I will return later."

"I said come in." Mr. Deighton's voice was gruff.

Griffith entered the house and followed the man as he limped into a parlor. The wallpaper was faded and peeling. The furnishings and carpet were worn, but tidy.

Mr. Deighton took a seat on the sofa and gestured for him to sit on a nearby chair. Griffith complied.

"I'm sorry I can't offer you tea," Mr. Deighton said. "Mary, my daughter-in-law, is nearing her time of confinement. And Eloise is out doing the shopping. Now, Mr.?"

"Hastings," Griffith supplied. "Griffith Hastings."

"Mr. Hastings, tell me how you know my daughter."

"She found Victoria on the promenade…."

"No, not that. You tell me how you knew her ten years ago. You did know her, didn't you?"

Griffith ran a finger under his collar, which was suddenly tight. Beads of sweat formed on his upper lip, and he reached for a handkerchief to dab at his face. He had never planned on having this conversation with Eloise's father.

"Eloise…," he began.

Mr. Deighton frowned.

Griffith started again. "Miss Deighton and I met several years ago. We were acquaintances. Nothing more."

The man shook his head. "Acquaintances," he scoffed.

"You would almost convince me if I hadn't seen Eloise after you left. What did you tell her? What promises did you make?"

Griffith studied his hands. He didn't know Mr. Deighton at all, didn't know if he would be angry with Eloise over their secret relationship, even though it had ended years ago. It must not be easy for her, being a single woman. She needed support from her family, not conflict.

Mr. Deighton scrutinized his face as Griffith took a deep breath and straightened in the chair. He lost Eloise a long time ago, and he had nothing to lose now. While he still hoped he would get the chance to explain things to her, he knew that might not be possible. Whether he had any kind of future with her or not, he would not begin it with a foundation of lies. Not to her father, not to anyone.

"Your daughter and I met by chance, several years ago. We got to know each other over the summers when I returned to Whitby, and we formed an attachment. I had not reached the age of majority, but it was difficult to wait. I intended to return the next summer and ask her to be my wife, with your approval, of course. However, when the time arrived for me to return to Whitby, my father became ill. He made me promise that I would stay in London to care for my brother and mother, and that I would run the family business." Griffith did not say that he never dreamed his father would pass away. When he made that promise, he still had hope that his father would recover.

"When my father died, the family business fell to me. I was overwhelmed by the responsibility and by my grief. I could not break my promise to my father, so instead of returning to Whitby, I stayed in London to care for my mother and my younger brother."

He paused. "I never wrote to Eloise to explain, and that

was a mistake. I have regretted that many times over the years. She deserved better. I told myself that she would forget me and move on, and that I should do the same. My wife, Rebecca, was a family friend. On his deathbed, my father told me that he and Rebecca's family hoped that we would marry. Two years later, she became my wife."

A weight lifted off Griffith's shoulders. It was not the same as telling Eloise in person, but he was relieved to have finally told his story. He leaned back in his chair and waited for Mr. Deighton to respond.

"You are the one, then. The one who broke her heart. I have wondered, all these years. I figured it could not have been someone here in Whitby."

No matter what he'd told himself, Griffith had to own that he had been the one to break her heart. As he pictured her trusting blue eyes and her ready smile, he was stricken by the fact that he had been the one to take that away from her. And he could never give it back.

"I never meant to hurt your daughter," Griffith said. It was inadequate, he knew, but it was all he could offer.

"She did not take your failure to return well, Mr. Hastings. For weeks, I watched her running down to meet the train. Each day her hope lessened, each day her sadness grew, until she became a shell of herself. She didn't eat. She grew pale. She stopped going to the sea. I couldn't get her to tell me what happened. Her mother, either. Over time, she made the best of things. My Eloise is a strong woman. I hoped she would find someone to marry here, in Whitby, but no one captured her interest. After her mother died, her sorrow returned. I thought it would do her good to have a change of scenery, so I sent her to live with her aunt in London."

Eloise had been in London? The information caught Griffith off guard.

"When was she there?" Griffith asked, rising and pacing the room. They had never crossed paths, but knowing Eloise had been in London made him entertain thoughts of what might have been. If he had written to her the summer his father died, if she had known he still loved her, maybe they would have found a way to create a life together. Maybe he would not have married Rebecca. But then again, he would not trade Victoria for anything.

Mr. Deighton tapped his cane on the floor. "Eloise has been in London these past five years. She came home very recently. She is happy now and making a life for herself. I don't want her to be hurt again, Mr. Hastings. Whatever your intentions are in coming here today, please bear that in mind."

"I have no desire to hurt her again," Griffith said. And he meant it. They were both different now, and although he carried a memory of loving her that would not fade, he did not know her as the woman she had become. And she did not know him either. Perhaps too much water was under the bridge for either of them to want to move forward together. He had broken her heart once, and he did not wish to break it again.

"Will you give this to her for me?" Griffith handed Mr. Deighton a small package. "Please tell her that I came by to thank her. I won't bother you again, Mr. Deighton. Miss Deighton is…quite special."

When Griffith reached the door, he was surprised that Mr. Deighton offered his hand to shake in farewell.

"Pleasure meeting you, Mr. Hastings. I wish you and your daughter the best."

"Thank you, sir," Griffith said.

Mr. Deighton opened the door, and Griffith heard a familiar voice.

"You'll never guess what I found today, Father! New potatoes, peas, and cherries. And the mackerel was fresh off the boat. We shall have a feast tonight."

Standing there at the door with a basket on her arm was Eloise. When she spied him, the smile left her face, and she took a step back. Her face went white, and the basket began to slide.

CHAPTER 7

He was the last person Eloise expected to see upon returning home this morning. Griffith stepped forward and took the basket before she dropped it.

"Miss Deighton, I can explain," he said.

Eloise's heart was pounding, and she fought to gather her composure. She kept her voice even. "I'll thank you to leave, Mr. Hastings. You shouldn't have come."

"I came to thank you for finding Victoria, and to apologize," he said, but she held up a hand in protest.

"You have already thanked me, Mr. Hastings. If you'll please excuse me, I need to get this food inside."

He stepped aside and she brushed past him, hating the way her stomach flipped at his nearness. He handed the basket to her, and his hand brushed against hers as she took it. A knot rose in her throat, reminding her how much she had missed him. She frowned at her father. It was hard to imagine why he let Griffith in the house. What story had he told her father? She couldn't imagine what they had been discussing. Or maybe she could. At that, her insides quavered.

Eloise set the basket on the kitchen counter and removed her hat with trembling hands. Griffith and their history were all in the past, and she was determined to keep it that way. If she avoided him for a few weeks, he would realize that his memories of Whitby were grossly romanticized and not at all in keeping with the reality of the place, and she would be rid of him forever. It was for the best.

Taking the items out of the basket, she put them away. To her relief, she heard the front door close. Griffith was gone now. The uneven rhythm of her father's cane and footsteps warned her of his approach. She gripped the counter and exhaled slowly, bracing herself for whatever Father had to say.

"Are you all right?" he asked. "Mr. Hastings seems to have given you quite a scare."

Eloise managed a smile. "I wasn't frightened, only surprised. I didn't expect to see him again, especially not here."

She thought of the skinny boy running up the beach to retrieve his clothes on the day they met. The shy smiles he always gave her. The hesitant way he reached for her hand for the first time. No, she was not afraid of Griffith. But he had broken her heart. The only thing protecting that particular organ beating in her chest right now was the defense she had built by blaming him, making him the villain. And if she let him explain, if he proved to not be a villain, what would protect her tender heart then?

"What was he to you?" Father sat on a stool in the corner of the kitchen, placing both hands on his cane in front of him.

"What did he say?" Eloise asked.

"I have heard his version. Now I would like to hear yours."

"He was a friend," Eloise said. "We talked of being something more. I thought we had an understanding, but I was mistaken."

Father didn't press, and for that, Eloise was grateful. Griffith Hastings was a string of precious memories she kept tucked away. Pulling them into the light of day now would serve no purpose. And yet, he had been there. In her house. How many times had she dreamed of him coming back?

"You are a good daughter, Eloise. I only wish for you to be happy. After your time with Helena, are you certain you can be happy here?"

She didn't answer him as she put on an apron and mixed the ingredients for a pie crust. The familiar task of cutting the lard and flour together into fine crumbs and then adding cold water to form dough steadied her and soothed her aching heart. Because it did ache for him still. It didn't help that, despite the years and the scar on his cheek, he was as handsome as ever.

"I am happy to be home, Father," Eloise said. She divided the dough and rolled a crust, laying it carefully over the pie tin. She let it rest there while she made the filling.

"Mr. Hastings wants to talk to you."

Eloise paused, her hands holding the knife as she chopped ingredients for the filling. "I don't think revisiting the past is a good idea."

"Maybe you are right, but sometimes airing things out in the light of day is the best way to let them go," Father said.

Eloise raised her eyebrows at him in surprise. "You think I should speak to him? A married man with a child? I think it would do more harm than good."

"He did not tell you? He is a widower, Eloise. His wife died two years ago."

Eloise froze. She had not known that. Griffith had lost his wife, and Victoria had lost her mother. "That poor little girl," she said.

"You know what it is like to lose a mother. And you may not have lost a spouse, Eloise, but you lost someone you cared about. A shadow of that still follows you, even after all this time. Mr. Hastings was polite while he was here, but if you do not wish to speak to him, I will support you in that choice. He asked me to give this to you." Father set a small, brown package on the counter. "Now, I'm going down to the pier to wait for John. If he has a good catch today, I want to be there to help."

Eloise stared at the package as if doing so would make it disappear. Or move. Opening it might bring to the surface all the memories she worked so hard to keep tucked away. However, her curiosity got the best of her. She wiped her hands on her apron before picking up the package. It was square, and light in her hand. She couldn't imagine what would be in it.

Her fingers shook as she undid the bit of string and unwrapped the paper. Inside was a square of fabric embroidered with a seashell and her initials. A handkerchief. She traced a finger over the design. The seashell was fan-shaped, a scallop stitched in bands of white, yellow, and rust-colored brown. Her initials were in a deep blue floss.

When had he had this made? There hadn't been time between their meeting on the promenade and his visit this morning, unless he was skilled at stitchery himself. Eloise smiled at the thought of Griffith primly stitching. She knew that had not happened.

It occurred to her that if he had this tucked away these past several years, and had brought it to Whitby now, that he may have always intended to find her. The question remained: why was he seeking her out now?

Eloise tucked the handkerchief away and finished assembling the pie. The oven had been heating while she'd done the shopping and now she opened the door and tested the temperature. The coals had done their job, and she placed the pie inside to bake. She'd need to turn it during the cooking process, or it would be overcooked on the side closest to the coals and not done enough on the other side. But it would bake slowly all afternoon and be ready for dinner.

Father was right. She did have a shadow trailing after her, one that loomed larger in her mind now that she had seen Griffith. She picked up the broom, determined to sweep away any memories along with the sand that constantly invaded the house.

"Eloise!"

Startled, she dropped the broom, and it clattered to the ground. As she bent to retrieve it, Mary entered the kitchen.

"Didn't you hear me? Your mind must have been wandering." Mary ran her hand over her rounded belly.

"I am a little distracted today," Eloise admitted. "Is everything all right?"

"I am fine," Mary said. "I am torn between wanting this child to be born soon, and knowing that as inconvenient as this time is, it is easier to care for the baby while it is still inside me. I don't know how I shall cope with another little one to look after."

"I shall help you manage," Eloise said. It did not seem to be the right time to tell Mary that she wished to move out of the house. Mary and John had been so good to her. Besides, staying home to help Mary with the children would keep her out of Griffith's path.

"I'm so happy you are back," Mary said. "You are a great help to me. Now, tell me what has you distracted today."

"Let's sit in the parlor," Eloise said. She placed the broom in the corner of the kitchen and went to the other room. Mary sat down across from her. It would only be a matter of time before Mary teased the information out of her, and perhaps discussing her situation would help.

"Griffith was here, talking to Father."

Mary's face remained calm, as if Eloise were giving her an update on running into a neighbor at the shop. "I cannot believe he had the nerve to come here. What did he want?"

"He wants to speak with me."

"But you said he is married." Mary frowned.

Eloise shook her head. "Father said he is widowed."

"That is surprising news. How sad for him. But how are you taking this, Eloise? Do you wish to speak with him?"

"I am not sure that would be a good idea. I am planning to avoid him while he is here. Avoid him, and his daughter. He's had a whole life without me."

Mary squeezed her hand. "Yet he found out where you lived and came to see you. That has to mean something."

She showed Mary the handkerchief. "And he brought me this. What does it all mean, Mary?"

"Is the shell significant to you?" Mary asked.

Eloise shook her head. Shells were their secret code that indicated when and where to meet. But she'd never shared that with Mary, and she didn't want to, now. Somehow, it seemed like a secret that should be kept between her and Griffith.

"Maybe he gave it to you to finalize things. So much was left unfinished between you. Or perhaps he gave it to you because he hopes for something more," Mary said.

"I don't know about that, but I do know Griffith Hastings does not have power over my heart anymore," Eloise said. But even as she said it, she knew it was not the truth.

CHAPTER 8

Griffith wandered through Whitby, having no desire to return to the inn yet. His thoughts were filled with Eloise. She was just as beautiful as he remembered, even if she held herself at a distance. The cool exterior she projected, that of a proper lady, was both oddly appealing and strangely disquieting.

The thing he had always loved about Eloise was her sense of adventure. But when he'd seen her today, she was reserved. Where was the free-spirited girl he used to know?

While he did not regret going to her home and meeting her father, he was frustrated that he had not yet been able to explain things to her. He wanted to repair the damage he had caused years ago. He wanted to tell her that he had always loved her, and that he was sorry for the way things had ended between them.

Would the shell handkerchief mean anything to her? He'd had it made in London with every intent to give it to her as a token of his love for her. It had languished in the bottom of his drawer all these years. He hoped she would understand now that it was a memento of his feelings for her. He hoped that she didn't think it was her fault he hadn't come back. He needed to explain to her about the promises he'd made to his father. If he did so, she would at least understand the choices he'd made, even if she couldn't forgive him.

Griffith sat on a bench and lifted his gaze to the hilltop where the abbey ruins stood, silhouetted against the sky. As if pulled by some invisible cord, he found himself walking toward Church Street. It hadn't changed much. Brick shops and houses lined the street that rose steeply to the steps leading to the abbey.

Without hesitation, he climbed the steps. Whenever he came to Whitby with his family, they attended St. Mary's church on the hill. He loved exploring the ruins of the old abbey that rested nearby. At least once each summer, he and Eloise climbed over broken walls, scoured the ground for remnants of the past, and shared a picnic lunch in the shade of the old building.

Small birds flitted in the grass pecking at seeds as he entered the ruins. The abbey walls were silent keepers of many memories, including his. Griffith welcomed the memory as it sprang forth, fresh and vivid in his mind.

THAT SUMMER, when he was nineteen, he and Eloise met on the beach to swim whenever they could. All too often, Robert followed Griffith and interfered with their plans. But one night, late, they managed to steal away from their families and slip through the shadowed streets to the abbey steps.

He took hold of her hand as they climbed the steps in silence, stopping when they reached the cemetery at St. Mary's. Side by side, they watched the moonlight create a shimmering path across the harbor and cast a glow on the piers. A breeze carried the briny scent of the sea up to where they stood.

"I've lived here my whole life, and this view has never been more beautiful than it is tonight here with you," she said.

He wrapped his arms around her slim waist, drawing her close. "*You* are beautiful," Griffith said, pressing his lips against her hair. "Come with me."

The headstones were like sentinels around the church. When they entered the abbey ruins, Griffith pulled her into the shadows. She stood as still as a statue while he traced her lips with his finger.

"Eloise?" His voice was quiet, an unspoken question in her name. She responded by tilting her face toward him and reaching behind his head to twine her fingers in his hair. No one was here to interrupt them now.

He bent toward her and pressed his lips to hers. It was as if a million stars were twinkling inside him. He'd been longing to kiss her since that day in the sea, and it was worth every second of the wait. Her lips were warm and soft, and responded to his. He wrapped his arms around her, and she leaned into him. Never before had he felt so alive and so safe. He never wanted to be without her.

He pulled back after a moment, breathless. "Was it all right that I kissed you?"

Her smile shone in the moonlight. "I thought you were going to kiss me while we swam the day you came back. But then Robert interrupted us. I've been hoping you would kiss me ever since."

He caressed her cheek and kissed her once again. "I could get used to this. Perhaps someday we can make it a daily occurrence."

"Are you intimating that we have a future together, Mr. Hastings?" she teased.

"If you want one," he said. "I think we belong together."

She traced his jaw with her finger. "And what about your family? Will they object to you wanting to marry a girl like me?"

He caught her hand and kissed her fingertips. "How could anyone object to you?"

They'd walked back to town, saying little. When they neared the piers, she insisted that she could walk home alone. He hated to leave her, but she was adamant that they not be seen alone together so late. When he got back to the inn, he'd lain awake remembering the tenderness of her lips, the warmth of her in his arms. That night, he'd been determined to make her part of his life forever.

GRIFFITH REACHED out and laid his hand on the abbey wall. A stone broke free at his touch and tumbled to the ground. He picked it up and gently tucked it back into place. It stayed only a moment before falling to the earth again. This time, he left it alone. He and Eloise were earth and water. Sand and sea. He wondered if reviving their relationship would be as impossible as repairing the abbey walls. They were from different worlds, and yet when they were together, everything fell into place.

Realization swept over him. While he thought it had always been Whitby that made him happy, he was mistaken. Memories of Eloise surfaced in every part of town. It was not Whitby that made everything special, but his time with her. When he was with her, he was brave enough to dive down in the sea and search for shells, adventuresome enough to traverse rocky beaches hunting for fossils, free enough to escape his mother's watchful eye and go exploring. Around her, he was more himself than he was around anyone else.

Being with her brought out the very best in him. It wasn't that he belonged in Whitby, it was that he belonged with Eloise.

Somehow, he had to see her, get her to listen to him, explain to her that despite everything, he had never stopped loving her. If he apologized for leaving her all those years ago, maybe she would still reject him, but it was a risk he had to take. He didn't deserve a second chance, but he clung to the hope that she would give him one.

CHAPTER 9

$\mathcal{E}$loise awakened to a gentle knock on her bedroom door. She pulled on a dressing gown over her night shift before opening it. John was fully dressed, ready for a day of fishing.

"What's wrong? Is it Mary?" Eloise asked.

"She's asleep, but she had a restless night. I am uneasy about leaving her alone. Will you be close by today?"

The lines and creases on John's face were more pronounced this morning. Eloise placed her hand on his arm. "I plan to be here all day. I'll make some breakfast and make sure the children don't disturb her so she can rest. Everything will be fine."

"Thank you," John said. "I knew I could count on you."

Eloise dressed quickly. A light rain fell against the windowpanes as she entered the kitchen. Hopefully the fishing would be good this morning. Eloise lit the coals and prepared breakfast.

By the time Mary entered the kitchen, Eloise had dressed and fed Johnny and Thomas.

"You should've wakened me." Mary stifled a yawn.

"Don't be silly," Eloise said. "You'll be losing enough sleep when the new baby arrives. Sit and eat." She filled a plate and placed it on the table.

Mary sank gratefully onto a chair. "Mother said she would make us a pigeon pie today. I hate to ask it of you, but would you fetch it from the inn?"

Eloise knew Mary's parents ran the Seaside Inn, and she did not want to go anywhere near it. The Hastings used to stay there when they had come in the summer, and now that they were back, she didn't want to risk running into Griffith. Still, Mary was so uncomfortable as her time drew near that Eloise could not refuse the errand.

When the morning work was done and the children were settled, Eloise collected a basket for the food and an umbrella for the rain. Johnny and Thomas trailed after her.

"Can we go with you? Please?" Johnny asked.

The weather would keep many people from the promenade and the beaches today. They would, instead, seek shelter inside. It would be difficult enough to make her way through a crowded inn without two children in tow.

"Not this time," she said. "But if you are very good for your mother while I am gone, I will help you build a tower with your blocks later."

"We'll be good," Johnny promised.

Raindrops pattered against her umbrella as Eloise headed to the inn. She hurried as much as she could on the slick street. When she reached the inn, she closed her umbrella and left it outside.

The dining area was indeed crowded with customers and abuzz with chatter. Thankfully, she did not see Griffith or Mrs. Hastings anywhere.

She made her way to the bustling kitchen where Mary's mother was hard at work, her cheeks flushed with effort, as she directed her staff in delivering food to their guests.

"Eloise! Did Mary send you? How is she doing?" Mrs. Lewis greeted her.

"She is well, but ready for this baby to come, I think."

Mrs. Lewis took the basket from Eloise and tucked a pigeon pie inside. She added some fish cakes, bread, and a jar of jam.

"Tell Mary that I shall be by to see her as soon as I'm able. It is such a blessing that you are there with her."

"I am happy to help. Thank you for the food," Eloise said. She carried the basket through the bustling dining area. The rain was lessening, and weak sunlight peeked through a break in the clouds. Lost in thought, she didn't see Victoria coming down the stairs.

"Eloise!" Victoria rushed to her and wrapped her arms around Eloise's skirt.

Somehow, she managed to keep her balance. She patted Victoria's shoulder. "It's nice to see you again," she said, and was surprised to find that it was true. But Victoria would not be here alone. She glanced around the room and spotted Griffith and Mrs. Hastings near the stairs. Eloise wished she could escape without having to see them. Her only encounter with Mrs. Hastings, ten years ago, had not been pleasant. To her dismay, Mrs. Hastings headed in her direction.

"Victoria, set this woman free." She reached for the girl.

"She is no bother," Eloise said.

Griffith cleared his throat. "Mother, this is Miss Deighton. Miss Deighton, this is my mother, Mrs. Hastings."

Eloise waited for the woman's reaction to the introduction. Did Griffith know that she had met his mother many years ago?

"It's nice to meet you," Mrs. Hastings said.

Their meeting was to remain a secret, then. It seemed Mrs. Hastings had not told Griffith about their earlier encounter. Aunt Helena's advice flashed through her mind.

When you are in an uncomfortable social situation, be polite, even if you must lie.

"It's a pleasure to meet you, Mrs. Hastings," Eloise said.

Was it her imagination, or did a flash of guilt cross the woman's face? Eloise turned her attention to Victoria. "I'm sorry I don't have more time to talk to you right now, but I hope you are enjoying your stay in Whitby."

"We are quite busy also, Miss Deighton," Mrs. Hastings said. "As soon as the rain clears, I've made arrangements for Mr. Hastings to meet a lovely young lady on the promenade." Her gaze swept over Eloise, and she sniffed.

Eloise was keenly aware of the simple day dress she was wearing. Why, when she ran into Mrs. Hastings, did it have to be under these circumstances? It was as if the previous years had never happened, as if all her work to become a lady worthy of the Hastings family didn't matter. Mrs. Hastings still preferred another woman over Eloise as a possible match for her son.

Victoria tugged Eloise's arm. "Do you like my necklace? Grandmama bought it for me."

A delicate strand of black beads hung on either side of a heart-shaped pendant. Eloise had a similar necklace at home. Father had given it to her when she left for London, to wear to remember her mother.

"It's lovely," she said. "I have one very much like it."

"Mine is to remember my mother," Victoria said. "She died. Did your mother die, too?"

Mrs. Hastings coughed in her handkerchief. "Victoria!"

Eloise crouched down to the girl's level. "Yes. My mother died five years ago. I miss her very much."

"I miss my mother, too," Victoria said, her expression solemn. "But I was only four when she died. Sometimes it's hard to remember things about her. Does that happen to you?"

"Yes. But when I wear my necklace, it reminds me of her."

"Come along, Victoria. We must let Miss Deighton get on with her errand. The rain is stopping, and we shall visit the sweet shop after lunch while your father is on the promenade."

Eloise turned to Griffith, who had remained silent through the whole encounter. Mrs. Hastings was watching them. Despite the fact that he'd introduced her to his mother, would it be uncomfortable for him if she brought up his visit to her home? She decided to find out.

"It was very thoughtful of you to bring me a gift, Mr. Hastings." Eloise took some satisfaction from Mrs. Hastings' startled expression.

To her surprise, Griffith did not seem embarrassed. In fact, his jaw twitched as if he were hiding a smile. He laid a hand on her arm.

"It is a small token of my gratitude. I would like very much to meet with you, Miss Deighton. Someplace where we might have a conversation. There are so many things I need to say."

Eloise fingered the cloth covering the basket of food. Her thoughts darted to all the places where she and Griffith used to meet: the beach, the abbey ruins, the cemetery by the church. She had no desire to sneak off to any of those places to meet him now. Not only were they too full of memories, but she doubted any of those locations would meet with his mother's approval. She was also annoyed that she still cared what his mother thought. Eloise was torn between keeping Griffith firmly in her past, and a new desire to find out what he had to say.

"I don't wish to meet you in secret, Mr. Hastings. We are no longer children." She raised her eyes to meet his. She could still get lost in those green eyes.

"No more secrets," he said. "I am happy to meet you wherever you would like."

Her heart jumped at the thought of being with him out in the open. That was something he had never wanted to do in the past. But she must not read too much into it. Perhaps Griffith thought one simple meeting might be all that was required to lay the past to rest.

"The Tea and Tides has a lovely menu. I could meet you there tomorrow," she said.

Griffith's expression brightened. "Tomorrow at noon?"

"Yes," Eloise said. "I shall see you tomorrow."

He thanked her, and Eloise left the inn, hurrying home. She arrived to find Mary settled in a chair in the parlor while Thomas and Johnny played nearby. The boys sailed their wooden boats over imaginary seas.

"Was Mother very busy?" Mary asked.

"Yes, the inn was crowded. She said she would be by to see you soon."

"And did you see anyone else while you were there?"

Eloise was not about to tell Mary that she had seen Griffith, but the heat rising in her cheeks was a dead giveaway.

"You saw him," Mary said.

"Yes." Eloise kept her tone light.

Mary leaned back in the chair. "It's so tiresome to be stuck here all the time. Give me details."

Eloise shrugged. "There isn't much to tell. He was there with his family, and I said hello to his daughter." She was reticent to tell Mary about meeting with Griffith tomorrow. Until she heard what he had to say, and until she determined what impact that had on her feelings for him, she wanted to keep it to herself.

CHAPTER 10

Griffith arrived at the Tea and Tides well before noon the following day. He chose a table with a view of the street and ordered tea while he waited. She would come. He hoped she would.

He'd paid particular attention to his appearance today. Nothing could be done for the scar on his cheek, but his hair was combed, and his shoes were shined. Not that Eloise would notice. She had never cared about appearances before. Reaching into his pocket, he pulled out the little shell he'd brought back to Whitby. He set it on the table, planning to give it to Eloise when she arrived. They had used it to communicate years ago, and he hoped it would break the ice and help them talk now.

He wanted to tell her what she meant to him. His life in London was controlled and very safe. Then he met Eloise, and his world changed. She was fearless. It seemed natural to explore with her, not reporting his every move to his mother. After his father died, the challenges of keeping the business going and overseeing Robert's education were often too great. Many times, he'd drawn on the memory of Eloise's fearlessness to find his own courage.

Minutes ticked by, and she did not arrive. Had giving her the handkerchief been a mistake? But she'd brought up the gift in front of his mother, and she'd agreed to meet with him. He didn't imagine she would do that if she didn't want to see him.

He waited and watched for her, spinning the shell on the table. The hands on his pocket watch indicated it was one o'clock and his second cup of tea had grown cold before he finally decided to leave. He tucked the shell into his pocket.

How many times had she waited for him on the beach ten years ago? Perhaps this was a message from her to let him know she had no interest in seeing him again. Disappointment swelled inside him.

If she never wanted to see him again, he had to respect it. He would focus on Victoria and their time here together, on creating new memories with her in Whitby. He hoped being here would help him cope with the pain over losing Rebecca, and it had. What he had not counted on was how much being here made him want to be with Eloise. Even now he remembered the touch of her hand, the tenderness of her lips against his. He walked out of the café and scanned the street on the slim chance that she was very late. But he did not see her anywhere.

The sweet shop was nearby, and he went inside. Victoria had not yet tried the local Whitby rock, a spearmint-flavored stick of candy. And Mother had taken a liking to chocolate. He chose treats for both of them and made his purchases.

On the way back to the inn, he spotted the small niche in the sea wall where he and Eloise used to leave shell messages for each other. As he expected, the niche was empty. He took the shell from his pocket and rubbed it between his thumb and forefinger. Was he ready to part with it? If she saw it in the niche, maybe she would meet with him and give him one more chance. If she ignored it, maybe it was time for him to leave the shell back where it belonged.

He set the shell in the hollow and walked away. Leaving it was probably futile, but he knew he would check the spot each day until he left Whitby, hoping she would leave a shell for him signaling they could meet. But if she did not want to meet with him, he would not press the issue. Now it was up to Eloise.

CHAPTER 11

*E*loise checked her appearance in the mirror. She'd pressed her best dress, and the blue fabric brought out the color of her eyes. Her hair was carefully coiled and pinned beneath her hat. She pulled on her gloves, ignoring the tremble in her hands. In a few minutes, she would be with Griffith at the Tea and Tides.

Aunt Helena always said that for a woman to survive in society, she must be an actress. But in private, a woman must be true to herself. Today, with Griffith, she was prepared to be an actress. That was how she would survive this encounter.

She slipped downstairs unnoticed by anyone in the family. Opening the front door, she took a deep breath to calm herself. The idea of meeting Griffith for lunch brought feelings of both excitement and dread. The piece of her that missed him couldn't wait to see him, but the part of her that had been so lost without him didn't want to take the risk. Before she could step outside, Mary groaned from the bedroom.

"Eloise, I need you!"

Mary had been fine when they ate breakfast earlier. But that was hours ago, and she wouldn't be calling if it weren't urgent. Eloise did not hesitate. She closed the door and rushed upstairs, removing her hat and gloves as she went.

The air in the bedroom was stale and the curtains were drawn. Eloise went to Mary's bedside.

"Thank goodness you are here. The pains are strong. Could you help me change and get to the birthing bed?" Mary asked. She was overcome by another contraction as Eloise took her hand.

When the pain subsided, Eloise helped Mary over to the bed set up in a corner of the room. It had belonged to Eloise's mother but was handed down to John and Mary when Johnny was born.

"John is out fishing. Can Father get the midwife?" Mary said.

Eloise poured water into the wash basin and dipped a cloth in it. As she wiped sweat from Mary's face, she tried to be reassuring. "I think Father went to the fish market to visit his friends. I'll have to go for the midwife. Will you be fine until I get back?"

Mary grit her teeth. "I think I can manage if you hurry."

Eloise brought over the shift and petticoat Mary had set aside to wear during delivery.

"Let's get you changed. Did you know that in London, women are giving birth in the hospital?"

"I'd rather be here than in a hospital filled with strangers."

A loud thump came from downstairs, followed by a wail.

"That sounds like Thomas." Mary struggled to rise from the bed.

"I'll check on him," Eloise said. She hurried downstairs to find Thomas on the kitchen floor next to a toppled chair. His face was scrunched and tears rolled down his cheeks.

Eloise scooped him up, kissing his blond curls. "You're all right. That's a big boy."

"I want Mama," he said, wiping at his face with a chubby fist.

"She's upstairs having the baby, and she can't be with you right now," Eloise said. "Where's your boat? Let's find Johnny to play with you."

"I'm hungry," he said.

Eloise found bread, jam, and leftover fish cakes and arranged the food on plates for Thomas and Johnny. Johnny climbed on a chair and began eating, but Thomas needed help. Time was ticking away and with it, her chance to meet Griffith. Even if she ran to fetch the midwife, she would not be back in time to go to the Tea and Tides. She had no way to get word to him.

Mary cried out. Thomas, a look of alarm on his face, wiggled off his chair. Eloise stopped him from racing upstairs and returned him to his seat.

"Your Mama is all right," she said. "Don't be afraid. Soon you'll be a big brother. Right now, you can help your mother by eating your food." She placed her hand on Johnny's shoulder. "I need you to watch him while I go get the midwife. Can you do that for me?"

Johnny nodded and took another bite of food. Eloise went back upstairs to Mary.

"Is Thomas all right?" Mary asked.

"Johnny and Thomas are eating. They'll be fine for a few minutes while I go for the midwife."

Mary focused on Eloise. "You are all dressed up. Were you calling on someone this afternoon?"

Eloise smoothed her skirt. "I wanted to go for a walk."

Reaching for Eloise's hand, Mary shook her head. "A walk? Not in that dress. You were meeting Griffith, weren't you? I'm sorry, Eloise. This is terribly inconvenient for you."

"You and the baby are the most important thing. I'll see Griffith another time," Eloise said.

She didn't know if she would get another chance to meet with him, but maybe it was for the best. No matter what he had to say, she doubted it would change anything between them. He'd made his choice long ago, and it hadn't been her.

The door to the house creaked open and she heard her father's voice downstairs. Eloise left Mary and hurried to greet him.

"I need you to get the midwife," Eloise said.

"It's her time, is it? I'll hurry."

Time dragged as Eloise waited for Father to get back. She put the kettle on the stove, changed into a day dress, and kept an eye on the boys and on Mary. When Father returned with the midwife, it was with tremendous relief that Eloise ushered her into Mary's bedroom.

More than an hour had passed since she was supposed to meet Griffith. Eloise was certain he was not waiting for her any longer. She hid her disappointment as she left Mary and went downstairs.

"How is she?" Father asked.

"She's fine," Eloise said.

"It shouldn't be long," Father said. "I think it goes quicker each time. And Mary had no trouble with the first two."

"I hope everything goes well. But with another child in the house, it's getting crowded. I think it's time that I secure lodgings of my own. I could find a room nearby."

Father grunted. "People will talk. It is not right for a woman to be on her own. You shall stay here with your family until you are married."

"And if I never marry?"

"This is your home," he said.

Eloise sighed. While she appreciated that Father would always have a place for her, she missed the freedom she'd had with Aunt Helena. It was too easy here, in the home she'd grown up in, to fall back into old patterns of trying to be like her mother and falling short.

When John finally came home, he had a new baby daughter to greet him. Mary was resting upstairs with the baby snuggled in her arms. Eloise followed John to see the little one.

He crossed the room and gave Mary a kiss, stroking the baby's head. "What shall we call her?"

Mary smiled at him. "I'd like to call her Eloise. I want her to grow up independent and adventurous like your sister."

Eloise was stunned. Mary wanted to name the baby after her? She blinked rapidly to fend off tears.

John smiled. "I think that is a fine idea. Eloise it is, and we will call her Ellie."

After the midwife left, John took coins from his pocket and handed them to Eloise.

"Mary wants an ice. Would you get them for all of us to celebrate?"

Eloise didn't give a thought to her appearance, and only when she was approaching the vending cart did she notice she was bareheaded, and that her day dress was rumpled. It couldn't be helped. She ordered six penny ices and then wondered how she would carry them all. As she turned to leave, carefully balancing her precious load, she heard familiar voices.

"I want an ice." Victoria pointed to the vending cart.

"Not right now," Mrs. Hastings said.

"Where's Papa?"

"He did not say, but I hope he has gone to meet a nice young lady."

Victoria stomped her foot. "He promised to take me to the beach."

Mrs. Hastings cleared her throat in disapproval.

"Your father gets lonely, Victoria. It is appropriate for him to socialize with people his own age."

"I don't want another mother. I want to go swimming, and I want an ice," Victoria said.

Mrs. Hastings gripped Victoria's hand. "It is an unfortunate fact of life that we cannot always have what we want."

The truth of that statement hit Eloise hard. Ice cream dripped on her hand, and she knew everyone was waiting for her in the Deighton household. As she hurried home, her heart ached for Victoria. It was understandable that the child did not want anyone to replace her mother. It hadn't been easy for Eloise when she lost her own mother, and she had been a grown woman. She could not imagine how hard it must be for Victoria. And now Griffith was out meeting other ladies. Victoria didn't like that, and Eloise discovered that she didn't like it, either.

As she passed the sweet shop, she glanced at the sea wall out of habit. The niche was always empty, and she chided herself for continuing to check it after all these years. But today, something white was in the hollow.

It was a shell, like the ones Griffith used to leave her. Eloise nearly dropped the ices. Griffith could not have put it there after she missed their meeting, could he? Maybe someone else set the shell there. It was a natural place to tuck a treasure. Surely a child had hidden it. Not Griffith.

But it was a small, white scallop shell. If it were from Griffith, maybe it meant he still wished to meet her even though she had not come today. Maybe she would have the chance to talk to him after all.

Aunt Helena once said to her, "When your mother chose to marry your father, she told me love is always worth the risk. If you get the chance at love, you should always take it."

Aunt Helena had been widowed for a long time when Eloise went to live with her. But like Eloise's mother, she had married for love. Aunt Helena always said her time with Uncle George, no matter how brief, was time she treasured.

Eloise stepped closer to the shell tucked in the sea wall. The truth was, seeing Griffith reminded her that during the time they'd spent together, he always accepted her exactly how she was. When she first met him, she was awkward, a wild child running around Whitby. Her older brother, John, was a fisherman like their father. He had confidence in his place, while Eloise, who was not as refined as her mother, was never quite certain how she fit. But she always fit with Griffith.

Not only was he back in town, but he'd given her that seashell handkerchief. One he had to have had made for her in London. He'd introduced her to his mother, and she'd met his daughter. Griffith used to be her friend, and she owed it to her younger self to hear what he had to say. That Eloise, the one who had been left behind, deserved to know the truth.

Eloise rushed home with the ices and delivered them to the family. She didn't wait to eat hers but instead handed it to John and hurried upstairs to fetch the little purple shell from her trunk.

"Where are you going?" Father asked.

"I have an errand. I'll be right back," Eloise said. It wasn't proper to run down the cobblestone street back to the sea wall, but she walked as quickly as she dared. Once she reached the niche, she paused, hands trembling and heart racing.

If she put the purple shell in the hollow and took the white one, it left the message to meet on the beach in the morning for a swim. But if she left her shell with the white one, it meant they would meet in the morning at the abbey ruins. Her hand shook as she placed her purple shell alongside the white one and headed for home. Morning could not come soon enough.

CHAPTER 12

When Griffith returned to the inn, Victoria and Mother were seated on a bench outside. Victoria's cheeks were sticky with ice cream.

"Were you on the promenade?" Mother asked.

"No. I went to meet with Miss Deighton, but she never came."

Mother's jaw tightened. "Miss Deighton? Whatever for? I fail to see what either of you would have in common."

Griffith hadn't ever told Mother about Eloise. That he had known her for years, and that at one time, he had planned to marry her. To her, Eloise was simply a local woman he had just met, not an old friend. She would not understand at all why he wanted to spend time with her.

He fidgeted with his cuffs. He was reluctant to discuss Eloise with his mother, but he would not lie about her. "Miss Deighton and I have more in common than you think."

"I hope you are not planning to reschedule. I've arranged for you to walk on the promenade tomorrow with Miss Northrup and her mother."

Griffith frowned. The last thing he wanted to do was

meet another woman. "I wish you would not interfere with my social life, Mother."

"It is not interfering. I have merely arranged for an introduction. The Northrups do not live too far from us in London, and if you find some things in common, perhaps you will wish to meet again when we are back from this trip."

He sighed. "I will meet with Miss Northrup on the condition that you do not make arrangements for me to meet anyone else while we are here. But since I was not able to meet with Miss Deighton today, my afternoon is free. What shall we do?"

"I want to swim!" Victoria said.

Griffith smiled and stroked her hair. "That's a fine idea. But I am not allowed to swim with you. I have to stay in the men's section, and you have to swim with the ladies."

Victoria turned to her grandmother. "Will you take me?" she asked, a hopeful expression on her face.

"Don't you think she is rather young to go for a swim?" Mother asked.

"I'm old enough," Victoria insisted. "We could share a bathing machine."

Her grandmother's face blanched. "I have no desire to get in the water. Your father may take you wading by the shore. I think that will be plenty for you this time."

Victoria was crestfallen, but Griffith lifted her chin. "I promise you that you shall swim in the sea if that's what you truly want. But it might not be today."

Victoria rewarded him with a hug. Then she clasped her grandmother by the hand.

"Please Grandmama. You'll be able to tell everyone that we swam like Queen Victoria."

"I am not Queen Victoria, and I will not swim. You should not encourage her, Griffith. She cannot go in a bathing machine alone, and it is not appropriate for you to accompany her, so I believe this matter is settled. I shall be in my room if you need me." Mother retreated inside the inn.

"If we can't swim, what will we do?" Victoria asked.

Griffith took her hand. "I know just the thing." He led her to the promenade, where she hung back.

"I don't want to get lost again."

We won't go far, and I promise I won't let you out of my sight."

She tightened her grip on his hand as they walked. Soon they reached the edge of the square. The band was not playing at the moment, but a booth was set up nearby with a Punch and Judy show. He and Victoria found a spot with a good view of the puppet stage and sat on the grass. She cuddled next to him and, to his delight, laughed at the antics of the puppets.

"I wish we could always do things like this, Papa."

"I do too," Griffith said.

"Do you really have to meet those ladies tomorrow like Grandmama said?"

"It will make your grandmother happy if I do."

Victoria jutted out her lower lip in a pout. "It won't make me happy."

"Sometimes we have to do things we don't want to do," Griffith said. "Grandmother has done so much for us, I will do this one small thing for her, and then you and I will spend the rest of our time here together."

"Promise?" Victoria said.

He got to his feet. "I promise. Come, let's get ready for dinner."

THE NEXT AFTERNOON, Griffith accompanied Mrs. Northrup and her daughter, Miss Evangeline Northrup, on the promenade. It was busier than usual. Tourists filled the benches and gathered in the open square to listen to the band. He found the whole thing slightly tedious. Ten years ago, he never spent time on the promenade. He and Eloise always found something more interesting to do.

"Don't you agree, Mr. Hastings?" Miss Northrup asked.

Griffith was caught wool-gathering, much to his chagrin. He tried to recall what Miss Northrup had been talking about but could not remember.

Mrs. Northrup glared at him. "Evangeline was saying she does not plan to try a bathing machine while we are here. She does not fancy a swim as the sea hardly seems sanitary or appropriate for a lady. Have you been swimming, Mr. Hastings?"

"Not this season. But I used to swim often as a boy. The sea is marvelous. You should try it while you are here. I'm sure the bathing machines are perfectly safe."

Miss Northrup clearly lacked Eloise's spirit of adventure. Eloise never found the sea unsanitary, and she had grown up swimming freely, without the use of a bathing machine.

"You used to swim often? And you never became ill?" Miss Northrup asked.

He decided to have a bit of fun with them. "I never became ill from swimming. And it is quite charming to swim alongside the fish. Get acquainted with your dinner, you might even say."

Miss Northrup squealed and tightened her grip on her parasol. "You have seen fish while you were swimming? I wouldn't like that at all!"

Griffith wished Eloise were here to witness this conversation. She would find it humorous. "But where would the fish go while you are swimming? We enter their home after all. I might go out tomorrow. I have promised my daughter a swim while we are here in Whitby."

As Griffith walked near the beach with the cries of gulls in the air, he didn't care what the Northrups thought of him. Or what his mother would think of this conversation. Hopefully, she would respect his wishes and not attempt to arrange any more social engagements for him.

"Your daughter? How old is she?" Mrs. Northrup dabbed at her forehead with a handkerchief.

"She is six and eager to experience the sea."

"Six?" Miss Northrup's voice surprised him again with an even higher pitch. "That seems so young to swim. Are you sure it is a good idea?"

Griffith stopped walking and gazed out over the water. The bathing carts were busy today. The beach was crowded with families who had escaped the factories and city life to spend a day taking in the fresh air on the shore. Children wandered near the edge of the water, the timid ones running across the sand to avoid the waves. The ones who were brave let the water foam over their feet, laughing in delight.

"I think it is a tremendous idea," Griffith said. He waved his hand toward the children on the beach. "Look at them. What a wonderful day they are having!"

He should be there with Victoria, not here with the Northrups. He never should have agreed to this to appease his mother. The whole point of this trip was to give Victoria happy memories to fill the void in her life created by the absence of her mother. And how could he do that when he was not with her? He shouldn't be here walking with strangers. He should be with Victoria in the sand and the water.

"I'm sorry," he said. "I have lost all track of the time, and I need to get back to my daughter. It has been lovely to meet you, and I hope you enjoy your stay here in Whitby."

Leaving the Northrups, Griffith wove through the crowd as quickly as he could, rushing back to the Seaside Inn. If he wanted Victoria to grow up with a sense of adventure, he would have to be the one to teach her. His mother would not be the one to do it. She would raise Victoria as he had been raised—to follow the rules and do what was proper.

And he was tired of being proper.

When he arrived back at the inn, he knocked on the door of Victoria's room. Mother opened it. "You're back early," she said, disapproval in her tone.

"Victoria! Let's go to the beach!"

"Really?" Victoria popped into view, a wide smile on her face.

"Yes. We'll take off our shoes, get sand in our toes, and meet the waves at the edge of the sea."

"Griffith! It is time for Victoria to rest and then we shall need to wash up and dress for dinner. You mustn't tire her out."

"No Mother, I *must* tire her out. That is why we came. She shall hear the calls of the seagulls and watch sand crabs burying themselves, and perhaps we'll find a shell or two. We shall stay until she has worn herself out exploring. I did not come to Whitby to walk on the promenade with strangers. I came to introduce Victoria to all the things I love here."

"Am I swimming today? Are we going in a bathing cart?" Victoria's eyes were round with hope.

"I should say not," Mother said. "I don't think you should be going to the beach at all. Nothing good will come from it."

"I disagree, Mother. I think everything good shall come of it. We shall return in time to get ready for supper and we shall work up an appetite while we are out."

Griffith went to his room and shed his hat, waistcoat, and tie. He had been so caught up in his old memories that he was failing to make new ones. Not this time. Not today.

Victoria skipped beside him as they walked to the shore. He carried a blanket and together they found a spot on the beach not far from the water. He spread out the blanket and they sat to take off their shoes.

Victoria dug her bare feet into the sand and grinned at him. "Take me to the water." She stood behind him and wrapped her arms around his neck.

Griffith staggered to his feet and carried her on his back to the wet sand. He swung her down and held her hand as a wave approached. Victoria stepped backward as the water came near.

"Steady," he said. "It'll be a bit cold, but it won't hurt you."

The wave broke on the shore and raced toward them, becoming smaller and smaller until it rippled gently over their feet and retreated back to the sea.

"Again!" Victoria watched as wave after wave washed over her feet. Her feet sunk lower in the wet sand each time, and the smile never left her face.

"When may I swim, Papa?"

"If the weather is good, maybe we can go tomorrow," he said. "But we shall have to persuade Grandmama to take you."

"I wish you could take me."

Griffith sighed. "I wish I could, too. But men and women don't swim together."

"That's silly," Victoria said. Griffith had to agree.

When they tired of the sun and the sand and the water, Griffith brushed off Victoria's feet and helped her get her shoes back on.

"This day was perfect," she said.

Griffith kissed the top of her head. "Yes, it was. We will remember it forever."

As they walked back to the inn, they passed the sea wall, and Griffith checked the niche where he had placed the shell. He expected the shell to still be resting there alone. Or if not, he expected the hollow to be empty.

To his surprise, he saw a purple shell resting next to his white one. His pulse raced. It had to be from Eloise. She had not taken the white shell and replaced it with another. That was their code to meet on the beach. Adding a shell meant something different, and he frowned, trying to remember.

"When can we go up there, Father?" Victoria pointed to the abbey ruins on the hill.

The ruins. Two shells meant they were to meet at the abbey in the morning. When had she placed the shell there? Had she waited for him at the ruins today? He pocketed both shells, hoping she would take that as the signal to meet him tomorrow.

"Soon," Griffith said. "I'll take you up there very soon." But tomorrow morning, early, as the fishermen were heading out in their boats, he would go to the ruins to wait for Eloise.

hen Eloise checked on the shells the day after she left them, they were resting in the sea wall, untouched. Her heart sank, and she resisted the urge to collect both shells, take them home, and have a good cry. But the next day, when she checked again, the shells were gone. It had to be Griffith.

She rose early the next morning and dressed quickly, eager to meet him at the ruins. The morning air was cool with a slight breeze off the water as Eloise made her way to Church Street. Few people were stirring this early. The fishermen were readying their boats, but the shops were still closed, and the street was quiet.

She shivered as she walked up the hill. Whether the shiver was from excitement or the cool air, she could not tell. Her heart beat with a constant thrum…Griffith, Griffith, Griffith.

Willing her thoughts to still, she concentrated on climbing the steps. She must be patient. She would listen to what Griffith had to say and consider it carefully. Her mind told her to guard her feelings well, and over the years that she and Griffith had been apart, she had become adept at hiding her emotions. But now, her heart was insistent that she not keep it locked up anymore.

When she reached St. Mary's, she slowed. What would she say to him?

Nothing. She would not say anything until she heard what he had to say. Her breath caught in her throat when she saw him, leaning against the exterior wall. Tall and lean with broad shoulders, he was as handsome as he'd ever been.

Griffith waved as she approached. He waited for her to close the distance between them.

"You came," he said.

"I did. Are you surprised?"

"When you didn't come to the Tea and Tides, I wasn't sure you would meet with me."

"Mary, my sister-in-law, had her baby and I had to help. That's why I didn't meet you. I'm sorry."

Relief washed over his face. "How is she?"

"She is recovering well, thank you. And enjoying her new baby daughter."

"What did they name her?"

Eloise hesitated. "They named her after me."

"Ah, they must want her to grow up brave and strong like her aunt." He offered her his arm, and she took it. They walked into the ruins where the abbey walls hid them from view. It was so natural to be here with him, as if it had not been ten years since they were together.

He handed the purple shell back to her. "You should keep it. In case we need it again."

She accepted it and clutched it gently in her hand. Would she need the shell again? Only if things went well today. Despite her resolve to listen to him, she spoke first. "Where did you get the handkerchief?"

"I had it made for you in London."

"Ten years ago?"

"Yes. I planned to give it to you much earlier than I did. Eloise, please forgive me for not coming for you as I promised." Griffith faced her.

She remained silent.

"When my family didn't return to Whitby, I should have sent word to you. I'm sorry."

"I waited for you. Watched for you. Why didn't you come back?"

"A week before we were scheduled to return my father became ill. He made me promise that I would take care of Mother and Robert, and also keep the family business running. He died the next week, and I was overwhelmed. Time slipped away from me."

Eloise studied the ground, kicking at a pebble. Obviously, the death of his father would have kept him in London.

"I did not know about your father. I'm sorry. How old is Robert now?"

"He is twenty-five and recently married. We run the business together. He was away at school when Father died, and it was a very hard time for him."

"I know what it's like to lose a parent," Eloise said. "It must have been difficult for all of you. But you had that handkerchief made for me, you promised to come back, and instead you got married to someone else. How long did it take you to marry her after your father died?"

"I waited until I was out of mourning. A little over a year."

"Did you ever love me?" She fought, unsuccessfully, to blink back a tear.

He gently wiped it from her cheek. "I was trapped by my circumstances, barely twenty when Father died, and it was his dying wish that I court Rebecca. When my mourning ended, I convinced myself that you had forgotten me and moved on with your life. I'm so sorry, Eloise."

"That's her name? Rebecca? Tell me about her." She was afraid of what he might say, but she had to know.

"Rebecca was the daughter of my father's friend. When I began seeing her, it made my mother very happy. I don't know how it was for your father when your mother died, but my mother was laden with grief. When Rebecca and I married, it brought her some joy. Two years later, Victoria was born."

"How did she die?"

"In a carriage accident when Victoria was four."

Eloise saw the sadness that passed over his face and wondered if he would always carry it. "I'm sorry about your wife. Did you get your scar in the accident?"

"Yes, it's my reminder of that night." He touched the mark on his cheek.

His face was thinner now than it used to be. Fine lines creased his forehead, and she imagined each line carried with it the weight of his responsibilities. While Eloise did not agree with the choices Griffith had made, she understood why he made them. Her own grief had driven her away from Whitby, while Griffith's grief kept him tied to his home.

"You still have Victoria," she said.

"Yes. She was not with us the night of the accident and for that, I am grateful. It would have been unbearable to lose her."

The morning stillness hung thick between them and Eloise wandered deeper into the ruins. Griffith trailed after her. A question nagged her. "I wrote to you," she said. "Why did you never answer?"

His face paled. "I never received any letters from you." He paced before the crumbling abbey wall, running a hand through his wavy brown hair. "When did you write?"

"I wrote to you that summer when you didn't return. I thought we had an understanding about our future."

He reached out to grasp her hand, but she stepped back. He let his hand fall to his side. "Eloise, I swear to you that I never received your letters."

It clicked into place. Mrs. Hastings had to have intercepted the letters. "Your mother," she said.

"My mother?" His brow wrinkled.

"The evening before you left Whitby, I ran into your mother," Eloise said, the memory crystal clear in her mind. Griffith's mother, formidable and not used to being denied, accosted her on the street. Eloise was small before her, insides quavering. She could still hear the strident tone of the woman's voice.

"She warned me away from you. She must have suspected our feelings for each other, and she made it very clear that I was not good enough for you. She wanted me to have no contact with you ever again. But I couldn't stand it when you didn't return, and so I wrote. If you never received my letters, maybe it was because she didn't want you to see them."

Griffith picked up a stone from the rubble on the ground. With a groan, he heaved it out of the ruin and watched it arc through the air before landing out of sight. "If I had known," he began.

Eloise placed a hand on his arm, a jolt shooting through her at the contact. It was brazen, touching him that way.

"If you had known, then what? You would have written back to me? Would you have come back to marry me? Your father died, Griffith, and you had to stay with your family. We can't rewrite the past."

He leaned back against a wall. "You're right. I have told you about my years without you, but I know nothing of your life when we were apart. You came to London?"

She nodded. "After you stopped coming to Whitby, my mother became ill. I cared for her for a long while. She'd grown up in London and had an older sister there. When my mother died, Aunt Helena came to the funeral, and she asked me to accompany her back to the city to be her companion. Father encouraged me to go, so I did. I spent five years with her, and when she died, I settled her affairs and came home."

"You returned a lady."

"Yes," she said, flattered that he noticed the changes in her. "I'm not the girl swimming on the beach anymore." At least she was trying hard not to be.

Griffith leaned close, the warmth of his breath tickling her ear. "I miss that girl," he said. He took a step back as if he was waiting for her reaction.

Eloise nearly blurted out that she missed that girl, too, but she stopped herself. Did she want to be that girl again, running wild through Whitby? After her time in London, she was finally more like her mother. It was more than just her new wardrobe. She had changed. Now she understood that the world was larger than Whitby, and she had a greater appreciation for culture.

"I'm sorry I hurt you," he said. "I should have written and explained things. I should have gotten on a train and come to you. Can you ever forgive me?" His face was full of pleading.

Despite everything that had happened, he was still Griffith. Her Griffith. Both of them had made what they thought were the best possible choices under the circumstances.

"There isn't anything to forgive, Griffith. But you haven't answered my question. Did you ever love me?"

He did not hesitate, his eyes meeting hers. "More than I've ever loved anyone, Eloise. What happens now?"

She had imagined this conversation many times but wasn't sure how to answer him. What did she want now? For a moment, she was back at the ruins a decade ago. Her hand itched to run through his hair and her lips longed to feel his once again. What would it hurt? If she kissed him now, she would know if the spark between them was still there. It was possible that it had faded away long ago, and that all that was left between them was a memory.

She placed her hand on his chest and heard the sharp intake of his breath. His heart rate quickened beneath her touch, and he closed his eyes.

"I don't know what happens next," she said. Gently, she kissed the scar on his cheek. His jaw tightened, but he remained still.

She pressed her lips against his mouth, and he kissed her back. It was as if lightning flowed through her body. If anything, the connection between them was more intense than ever before.

"El," he said softly. He opened his eyes and searched her face.

"I still love you," she said. With that, she turned and walked away.

As she hurried down the steps away from the ruins, the weight of ten years of wondering and longing and missing him was gone, lifted off her shoulders as if it had never happened. But in its place was a storm of feelings that she wasn't sure how to handle.

She wished her mother were around to advise her. Or Aunt Helena. Maybe it was a mistake to kiss him, but at least now she knew that her feelings for him were unchanged. He was dear and familiar and still had her heart. But her life was here, helping her father. Griffith's life was in London taking care of his mother and Victoria. Those responsibilities kept them apart before, and now, their situations had not changed. Her brain could see no possible solution, but her heart ached to find one.

When Eloise entered the house, Father was waiting for her.

"You were out early," he said. "The boys are sleeping late this morning. Come to the parlor and keep me company."

Eloise followed him into the room and settled on a chair across from him.

"You've been to see him, haven't you?" Father asked.

"You said it would be good to talk to him." Eloise picked at a stray thread on the chair cushion.

"And was it?"

"You were right. I needed to hear what he had to say, but now I don't know what to do. I don't want to get hurt again."

Father hoisted himself to his feet and, leaning on his cane, crossed the room. He placed his hand on her shoulder. "The way I see it, you have two choices. You can walk away from him and never know what might have been between you, or you can see what happens if you give him another chance. It may work out, it may not. You may get hurt again. No one can foresee the future. What you have to decide is this: can you live with it if you never find out the answer?"

He walked out of the room, leaving her deep in thought.

CHAPTER 14

Eloise had kissed him. Of all the scenarios that played out in his mind before meeting with her, Eloise kissing him was not something he expected. He wanted to run after her, wanted to kiss her again. His stomach rumbled, reminding him that he had not yet had breakfast, and that Victoria would be waiting for him.

As he walked back to the Seaside Inn, he could not keep the smile from his face. Even before she kissed him, he knew that Eloise still had his heart. He must find a reason to see her again. And soon.

All these years, he thought that Mother didn't know about his relationship with Eloise. He had been naïve. She knew he went swimming many mornings, but had she guessed that he was meeting someone? Or had Robert told her about seeing him with a girl? Many times, he was late for dinner after meeting Eloise, his lips sticky from eating the ices they bought. He thought his secret was safe, but Mother had known.

When he entered the inn, Mother and Victoria were not yet in the dining area. Griffith went to his room and placed the white shell on his dresser. Victoria came to his room, her hair tangled from sleep, and Mother close behind her.

"Where were you?" Victoria asked. "You didn't answer when I came to wake you for breakfast."

"I'm sorry I wasn't here. I went for a morning walk," he said.

Mother pursed her lips. "Were you alone?"

Griffith shook his head, not wanting to discuss Eloise in front of Victoria. "I shall tell you later, Mother."

"It is time for breakfast. Let's brush your hair, Victoria," she said.

"I'll bring her down. Why don't you go ahead?"

Mother frowned but handed him the hairbrush. "I hope you know what you are doing."

Griffith suspected she was not referring to Victoria's hair. Meanwhile, Victoria went to the fossil on top of his dresser. She picked it up and her small fingers traced the spiral shapes. The rock held one raised fossil and one impression of a second creature.

"What is it?" she asked.

"It's called an ammonite," he said, scooping her up and setting her on the bed beside him. Victoria leaned against him, the fossil still in her hands.

"Ammonites lived in the sea long, long ago. Its shape is preserved in the rock," he said.

"Where did you get it?"

Griffith kissed the top of her head. "I found it on the beach with a friend many years ago. We split it open, and each of us kept half."

"Will you help me find one?" She hopped off the bed and placed the fossil carefully back on the dresser.

"Yes, I'll help you. We'll go to the beach this one came from."

"The beach with the bathing machines?"

"No, we'll need to find a beach with cliffs and rocks. And we'll need a hammer. I'll ask Miss Deighton about the best place to go. She'll know." Griffith wanted to see Eloise, and Victoria was providing him with the perfect reason.

"Can we go today?" she asked.

Griffith nearly corrected her to say, "May we go," as his mother would have, but he refrained. When he was in Whitby, following all the rules didn't seem as important. In fact, some of his favorite memories involved *not* following every rule.

"I don't see why not," he said.

The sun streamed through his window and shone on the ammonite. It was iridescent in the shaft of light.

He remembered all too well the day he and Eloise split the rock open on the beach, revealing the fossils inside. The way the rock split, leaving one fossil in relief and one indented in each half, was perfect. But more than the ammonite, he remembered standing close to her. A tendril of her hair had escaped in the breeze, and he'd tucked it behind her ear, his hand trembling.

As she had shown him how to set the oval-shaped rock on a boulder on the beach, how to place a chisel on the edge and hammer it, her hand touched his. The thrill that ran through his body at her touch ran through him again now.

He'd whispered promises to her that day on the beach, each of them taking half of the fossil. When he returned to Whitby he told her, they would reunite the halves.

I'll come back for you.

He could still picture her eyes, glistening, as they gazed into his. His fingers traced her lips. He tasted the hint of salt spray on her mouth when they kissed. His hands tangled in her long hair, pulling her close.

"Don't forget me," she'd said.

He hadn't forgotten her, and now he wondered if she still

had her half of the fossil. Would he ever get the chance to put the pieces back together? He hoped so. Until then, the ammonite mocked him from the dresser top.

He took the hairbrush and untangled Victoria's hair.

"Let's go find Eloise," Victoria said, tugging on his hand.

"Breakfast first. And you must remember to call her Miss Deighton," Griffith said.

"If I call her Miss Deighton, can we go find her after breakfast?"

"Yes. But first we need to buy a baby gift."

BY MID-MORNING, the streets of Whitby were bustling with locals preparing for the arrival of the first train of tourists. Griffith entered a shop with Victoria and Mother.

"Something simple, like a rattle or spoon, would be appropriate, I think, since you hardly know Miss Deighton or her family."

Griffith's cheeks flushed as he thought of the kiss he and Eloise shared earlier that morning. They were closer than he cared to admit.

Victoria chose a rattle, and the clerk wrapped it in brown paper.

"You and Victoria should continue shopping," Griffith said. "You don't need to help me deliver the gift."

"Oh, I believe that we do," Mother said. From her tone and meaningful glance, he suspected she knew something was going on between him and Eloise.

"You may come if you'd like to," Griffith said.

Victoria chattered happily as they walked to the Deighton home. Eloise opened the door when he knocked, her face lighting up when she saw him. But her expression changed when she noticed his mother and Victoria standing close by.

"Mr. Hastings. Mrs. Hastings. Victoria. How lovely to see all of you," she said.

Victoria grabbed the parcel from Griffith and handed it to Eloise. "This is for the baby, and we want you to tell us where to find annomites."

"Victoria!" Mother said. "Where are your manners?"

Eloise's gaze darted from Victoria to Griffith. He nodded, confirming the request. "I cannot remember how to get to the correct beach. Victoria would like to hunt for a fossil."

Amusement played across Eloise's face. "Have you a hammer? Or a chisel?"

Griffith shook his head. "No. We are not adequately prepared."

"It would be best if I came with you and showed you the beach. I am in possession of the tools you need."

He was only vaguely aware of his mother's eyes on him. His attention was focused on Eloise, the lilt in her voice, the hint of a smile on her lips.

"That sounds perfect," he said. Her eyes twinkled in response.

"Eloise is coming! I mean, Miss Deighton." Victoria clapped her hands in excitement.

"I have a few things to take care of here first, but I could meet you at the inn in an hour," Eloise said.

Mother stepped forward. "I believe we shall all be ready by then, Miss Deighton."

"I am looking forward to it, Mrs. Hastings," Eloise said, her eyes on Griffith.

"The more the merrier," he said with a grin. While having his mother along for their excursion was not his first choice, it was a small price to pay to spend more time with Eloise.

CHAPTER 15

$\mathcal{E}$loise regretted wearing her favorite pair of shoes.
They were more suited to a concert hall than a
rocky beach. Her attempt to impress Mrs. Hastings with her
fine clothes would fall short if she lost her footing. She was
nervous enough around the woman without the additional
worry about staying upright.

And it was awkward being around Griffith, too. Maybe
she shouldn't have kissed him at the abbey ruins. She gave
Victoria instructions about what to look for in the rubble on
the beach. As the girl scampered away, scrambling happily
amidst the rocks, Griffith drew near.

When Eloise slipped on a rock, he was there to steady
her, wrapping his arm around her waist and drawing her
close. She gripped his jacket to keep her balance.

"Are you all right?" he asked.

She nodded. She knew she should loosen her grip and
step away from him. Mrs. Hastings' sharp eyes missed nothing. And if Victoria saw them like this, what would she
think?

But Griffith's arm was warm around her. Comforting.

How easy it was to block out the world when she was with him. The birds, the waves, the other people. How easy it was to get lost in him once again. She fought the urge to lean into him, to press against him and wrap her arms around him.

Eloise stepped back. She gazed up at his face. His eyes were bright with longing.

"Thank you for catching me," she said.

"I didn't want you to fall. Those shoes are pretty, but not very practical. Not like those boots you used to wear." A smile flickered across his face.

He was teasing her, referencing their time together so many years ago. It was all so simple then. Meeting Griffith nearly every day without their families knowing.

Except somehow, his mother knew. Mrs. Hastings gave no indication that she remembered their encounter ten years ago, but Eloise had not forgotten it. And she would wager that Mrs. Hastings had not forgotten either. She hoped that today would change Mrs. Hastings' opinion of her, that the woman would somehow see her worthy of her son.

Griffith spoke again, his voice deep and quiet. "I wish we were here alone, like we were before. I still have my half of the ammonite. Do you still have yours?" His eyes were hopeful.

"Yes," she said. A gust of wind mussed his hair, making it stand on end. She reached up without thinking and smoothed the unruly lock. Her hand lingered. He caught it, bringing her fingers to his lips.

"Eloise," he whispered.

The sound of his voice saying her name made her melt. It was filled with pleading, longing, and promise.

When Eloise rested her hand on his cheek, he trembled beneath her touch. She took a shaky breath.

Griffith leaned closer, his eyes focused on her lips. She

closed her eyes, waiting for the sensation of his lips against hers.

"Griffith! Come see what Victoria has found!" Mrs. Hastings' shrill voice broke through the magic of the moment.

Eloise jumped. "You'd better go and see what she has."

Griffith swallowed hard, staring at her. "We have…unfinished business," he said.

"Yes, we do," she said.

Unfinished business indeed. Did she belong with Griffith? Her heart said yes, and she wanted to believe it. She wouldn't be here on the beach today if Griffith hadn't invited her. Fossil hunting and beach combing were a part of her. A part of her that she had set aside and that she missed. She was not sure how to reconcile her younger self with who she was now.

If you cannot find the place where you fit, you must create it, my dear, Aunt Helena used to say. Perhaps this was what her aunt meant: that she had to make room for all the parts of herself.

Eloise tore her eyes away from him and walked over to Victoria. "What did you find?" she asked, her voice too cheerful, too forced. It was hard to focus her attention on the girl. All she could think about was Griffith. Mrs. Hastings' steely gaze bored into her soul.

Griffith stood near her, his shoulder nearly touching hers. She could hardly bear his proximity. His finger brushed against her hand and curled around her finger. She closed her hand, keeping his finger tangled with hers, shifting so that Mrs. Hastings could not see.

The thrill of him ran up her spine like a flash of lightning. His hand was warm against hers. Even after all this time, his touch was familiar. Comfortable. As if they had never been apart. She was unprepared for the wave of emotions welling up inside her. She had been fighting the emptiness for so long, and now he was here, filling the void.

"Is this an annomite?" Victoria asked, holding up an oval shaped rock.

Victoria's pronunciation of the word made Eloise smile. It would be so easy to love this little girl. No wonder Griffith was smitten with her.

"Ammonite," Mrs. Hastings corrected.

Griffith rolled his eyes as if sharing a secret with Eloise. She surmised that he didn't approve of his mother's constant corrections of Victoria. Knowing they shared that opinion created another bond between them.

Eloise let go of Griffith's hand and took the rock from Victoria. "Get the hammer and chisel and let's open this." The child scampered off to fetch the tools that they'd set on a boulder nearby.

"Walk!" Mrs. Hastings said as the girl returned.

Although Eloise wanted to hammer the rock open herself, wanted to release the pent-up energy within her, she handed the rock to Griffith. Her instincts told her that Mrs. Hastings would not approve of Eloise wielding the hammer. Besides, Griffith should share this moment with his daughter.

He positioned the chisel along a barely visible seam in the rock and showed Victoria how to hit it with the hammer. Victoria took careful aim and gave the chisel a gentle tap. Nothing happened. She delivered a harder blow on the next try, and the rock cracked. Eagerly, she hit it one more time and the crack deepened. Griffith used the curved part of the hammer to pry the rock open.

Victoria squealed as the halves separated, revealing the remains of an ancient creature inside. It was one of the better ammonites Eloise had seen. She was delighted for Victoria, who picked up the fossil, studying it in wonder.

"Can I keep it?"

"May I," Mrs. Hastings said. Eloise glanced at Griffith who shook his head at the correction. She had to bite her lip to keep from laughing.

Griffith set the hammer down. "Of course you may keep it. Right, Miss Deighton?"

'Yes, it is yours," Eloise said. "It is a very fine ammonite, Victoria."

Victoria held both halves in her hands as if weighing something. "Do you have one?" she asked Eloise.

"Yes, I do," Eloise assured her, raising her eyes to Griffith. She thought of their ammonite, of the way the two halves were a perfect fit.

Victoria hesitated a moment longer before handing one half of the rock to her father. "You keep this one, and then we can always put the pieces together," Victoria said.

"That is an excellent idea." Griffith accepted the gift with appropriate solemnity. "I shall treasure it."

"I'm sorry I don't have one for you, Grandmama," Victoria said.

Mrs. Hastings' voice was brusque. "Thank you, but I have no need of such things. What would I do with a rock? Are we through here, now? Victoria and I should rest and freshen up before dinner. Perhaps you will spend the rest of the afternoon on the promenade, Griffith."

Eloise flinched. She didn't like the idea of Griffith parading around all afternoon where every visiting woman in town could attach themselves to him. She had to agree with Victoria—she didn't want Griffith to get a new wife, either. Yet, there was no reason to remain on the beach any longer. If she sided with Mrs. Hastings, perhaps that would gain favor with her.

"We could look all summer, and you wouldn't find a better fossil," Eloise said. "I agree with Mrs. Hastings. It is best if we get back to town." She collected the hammer and chisel and headed across the beach to the path that led back up to the road.

Eloise had a rock in her shoe, but she didn't want to give Mrs. Hastings the opportunity to disapprove of her by stopping to remedy the problem. It still stung--all those years ago when the woman informed her that she wasn't good enough for Griffith. When she practically commanded Eloise to stay away from him. In the weeks that followed the Hastings' departure from Whitby, she'd sworn to become so ladylike that when Griffith returned to claim her as his bride, even Mrs. Hastings would not be able to find any fault with her.

She'd done her best to change. She had the right clothes. She didn't run barefoot with her hair down anymore. She was more like her refined mother now than she had ever been.

Did Mrs. Hastings even notice? The woman hardly spoke to her, but then, Eloise hardly spoke to Mrs. Hastings. As they walked back to Whitby, she was determined to rectify that. How could Mrs. Hastings ever see her in a different light if she didn't show her who she had become?

"Are you enjoying your time here in Whitby, Mrs. Hastings?"

"It is a pleasure to see my son and granddaughter so happy. We had wonderful times here when Griffith's father was alive."

"I'm sorry I never had the opportunity to meet Mr. Hastings," Eloise said.

"He was a fine man." Mrs. Hastings walked briskly along the road.

Eloise struggled to come up with something else to say. "Life on the coast is very different from city life. But Whitby does have some advantages. Fresher air, I think."

She caught Griffith watching her, but she could not read his expression.

Mrs. Hastings made a very unladylike sound. "The smell of rotting fish is more like it. I don't care for it at all."

Eloise had the distinct impression that Mrs. Hastings would like to leave Whitby and all the memories surrounding it behind her. She would never convince Mrs. Hastings to love this place the way she did. It was best to change the subject. "Have you had an opportunity to hear the band playing near the promenade?"

"They were playing when Victoria was lost, but I did not stop to listen then. I had more important things on my mind."

"It must have been very worrisome when you were separated from Victoria," Eloise said.

"Yes, but all's well that ends well."

They reached the circular part of the road that led to the piers in one direction and branched off to the promenade or to Church Street in the other directions.

"I don't believe we will require your assistance again, Miss Deighton," Mrs. Hastings said. She took Victoria by the hand.

Eloise knew she was being dismissed, but she was reluctant to leave them. Now that Victoria had a fossil, she could think of no reason for them to be together again.

"Thank you for your assistance today, Miss Deighton. You have made Victoria very happy," Griffith said.

"It was my pleasure," she said, reluctant to leave him.

Griffith was eyeing her. He glanced at his mother. "Miss Deighton, given the chance, I should like to conclude our unfinished business from this morning."

Heat rose within her, flushing her neck and cheeks. It was no use pretending that she did not want to finish their business also. The thought of his lips on hers once again was nearly too much to bear. She would kiss him right here on the street if Mrs. Hastings wasn't standing nearby.

Griffith cleared his throat. "Perhaps I shall see you this evening on the promenade."

Mrs. Hastings frowned. His mother, it appeared, still did not approve of her. That had not changed. However, Griffith had changed. Every time he sought her out now, it was in public. He wanted to be with her out in the open, no matter what his mother thought.

"Is that an invitation?" she asked.

"It is indeed. Shall we meet at the Seaside Inn after dinner?"

"Yes, I'd like that." Even Mrs. Hastings' scowl could not stem the happiness flowing through her at his invitation. Her steps were light as she made her way home.

CHAPTER 16

Griffith tugged at his collar. It was nearly seven o'clock, but still light outside. He straightened his waistcoat and paced in front of the Seaside Inn, waiting for Eloise.

When she appeared, she was a vision in blue. Her dress was trimmed in black and the flounces of her skirt cascaded to the ground. The color contrast reminded him of the black rocks peeking out of the blue sea. It was perfect for Eloise. Her hair was up, and a large, stylish hat shaded her face. In this outfit, she would rival any woman on the promenade today.

She hesitated as she approached him, as if she were uncertain. Uncertain of what, he wondered. Her appearance? His reaction? He would leave no doubt in her mind.

"Miss Deighton," he said, tipping his hat. "You are the picture of elegance this evening."

Eloise's smile was his reward. "Why thank you, Mr. Hastings."

"Shall we?" He offered her his arm, and they joined the crowd strolling along the promenade. It was a struggle to keep his eyes off her. He'd always found her attractive, but today she took his breath away.

"It's a fine evening, is it not, Mr. Hastings?" She surprised him with a refined, upper-class accent, and it made it seem as if they were playing a game. He responded in a similar manner.

"It is, indeed, Miss Deighton. What shall we do to make the most of it?"

"Let us stroll with the wealthy, Mr. Hastings."

Griffith laughed. This was the way he remembered his conversations with Eloise—a touch of humor and no pretense between them.

Whitby was beautiful this evening. The abbey stood watch over the town from the top of the hill as the sun lingered in the western sky. The sandy beach stretched out alongside the promenade. Families who had come to Whitby for the day had packed up their belongings and headed home on the train. Griffith's attention, however, was not on his surroundings but on the woman who had taken his arm. "Did you ever imagine us like this?"

"All dressed up and walking on the promenade? Never. That was for grownups. Rich people. Not us. Well, maybe you, but not me. Not a fisherman's daughter," Eloise said.

"I never felt like I belonged here, either," Griffith said. "I am the son of a merchant. Father was self-made. All of our wealth came from his hard work."

They walked on, keeping pace with the other tourists. "I'm surprised your mother didn't come with us," Eloise said.

Griffith stopped by the cart selling ices. "She wanted to, but I needed her to stay with Victoria. Besides, I wanted to be with you without an audience, and it is perfectly acceptable for us to be seen together like this." He gestured toward the vendor. "Choose your flavor."

After Eloise chose chocolate. Griffith selected a green ice.

"I've become rather fond of cucumber," he said. "How is yours?"

Eloise peered up at him from under the brim of her hat. Her eyes sparkled beneath her long eyelashes. "See for yourself," she said, holding the glass toward him. He detected a playful tone in her voice. This was the version of Eloise he recognized. Not the formal woman she pretended to be, but a woman still filled with mischief and wonder.

Instead of taking the glass from her, Griffith placed his hand over hers and raised it to his lips. He slowly sampled the chocolate.

"Delicious." He released her hand. "Do you want to try mine?"

"I have tasted the cucumber before. While it is very good, I prefer the chocolate."

He shrugged. "Suit yourself." He had no desire to make Eloise feel uncomfortable today. Flirting with her was enough. Being here with her was enough. He had not felt this alive in a long time. The contrast between Eloise and his late wife was quite pronounced. Eloise was playful, fun, and always up for an adventure whereas Rebecca had been reserved and proper.

They finished the ice cream and returned the penny-licks to the vendor. He took the small glass jars from them and wished them a good evening. Eloise did not take Griffith's arm this time as they continued their stroll, and he missed the connection. When they reached the square, the band was playing.

"Let's stop," Eloise said. "The music is so festive."

Griffith stood as close to her as he dared, but not so close that he would bump into her hat. Still, he caught the scent of lavender from her skin.

The band played a lively, familiar tune and Eloise tapped her toes to the rhythm.

Emboldened by her presence, Griffith said, "Dance with me."

"What? Here? In front of everyone?" She shook her head, but did not protest when Griffith caught her hands and pulled her to an open space on the lawn.

He put one hand on her waist and kept her other hand in his, spinning her around. She tipped her face toward the sky. Her clear, lilting laughter was one of his favorite sounds as he led her through the dance. Before long, other couples joined in.

"You've changed," Eloise said, her blue-gray eyes fixed on his. "The Griffith Hastings I knew would never make a spectacle in front of strangers like this."

"I beg to differ. We are not a spectacle," he said, deflecting her observation. But inside he was thrilled that she noticed. He was not the strait-laced, play-by-the-rules person that he had been as a boy. He liked to think he had changed for the better.

"Do you remember the day we were swimming, and you wanted to jump off the rocks?" he asked.

"Yes. You were certain we would jump to our deaths, or at the very least, be seriously injured."

"I was terrified. I never did anything like that. You were the one who was always brave, always ready for adventure."

The band stopped playing and Griffith didn't want the moment to end. He wanted more time with Eloise in his arms. She didn't move away, and when the music started again, she squeezed his hand.

"You did jump off the rocks eventually," she said.

"I couldn't let you do it alone and have me be the chicken. It was exhilarating. We jumped at least twice more that day. You pushed me to face my fears, Eloise. You helped me grow into a stronger person, and I needed that strength when my father died." He blinked back his emotions.

"You've had so much loss," she said. "Your father, your wife."

"You have as well. Loss is a part of life."

"Indeed," she said.

A couple dancing beside them erupted into a shouting match. The woman placed her hands on the man's chest and pushed. "I saw you look at her!" she shrieked. "Did you think I wouldn't notice?"

The man stumbled and lost his hat. Picking it up, he brushed it off and placed it back on his head. He reached for the woman's hand, pleading with her not to make a scene, but she swatted his arm away.

Griffith led Eloise away from the arguing couple. She took his arm once again, and he placed his hand over the top of hers. "Let's never be like that," he said.

Eloise did not answer. For a moment, Griffith feared he had made a blunder. He implied that they might have a future together. Eloise might not be thinking the same. He glanced at her and was relieved to see her smiling.

"I don't think you have anything to worry about. I know you only have eyes for me," she said.

"Yes, it's true. You are, I confess, the apple of my eye. Tell me about your time in London. What did you and your aunt do to fill your days?"

Eloise's face lit up at the question. "Aunt Helena loved to go on outings. Exhibitions, performances, that sort of thing. We used to work in her garden together. She taught me that the hardiest plants flourish in the roughest places."

"On this we must agree. London is not an easy place, and yet you seem to have flourished there," Griffith said.

Embarrassed, Eloise ignored his comment and continued to speak of Aunt Helena and their activities. "She liked it when I read to her. We spent many evenings absorbed in books. She developed a fondness for Dickens and was terribly sad when he died."

"I much prefer the penny dreadfuls," Griffith said. "Particularly the highwayman stories."

"You do not!" Eloise lightly punched his shoulder.

"Ow!" Griffith rubbed his arm. He was rewarded with her smile.

"That did not hurt you," Eloise said. "And I don't believe you really read those."

"I do read them. They are easy enough to acquire at the train stations. When I was away from you, I had to find some way of having adventure in my life, even if it was through a story."

It was as if they had turned back the clock to a summer day a decade earlier. He relished this time with her. The evening was pleasant with only a few clouds in the sky. Shorebirds darted to the edge of the water and scurried away from incoming waves.

"Miss Deighton," he began.

"You always called me Eloise before," she said.

"Eloise, despite all the time that has passed, it is easy to be with you. As if we were never apart."

Eloise grew quiet beside him as they continued walking. They stopped at the sweet shop and Griffith purchased two sticks of Whitby rock, one red and one green. "For old times' sake," he said, handing a sweet to her. They sat on a bench and watched people walking by.

Griffith broke off a piece of the sweet and sucked on it. A rather large gull flew in and hopped at his feet, looking hopeful for some food.

When an older couple walked by, the man with a cane and the woman holding his arm, Griffith gestured to them. "I should like a love like that as I grow older. What about you? Have you ever wanted a family?"

She didn't answer right away, and he hoped he had not overstepped by asking her. When they were younger, they talked about their future together in vague generalities, but now he desired to know what she wanted in more specific detail.

"I always wanted a family of my own," she said. "But when I met a potential suitor in London, I did not love him the way I wanted to. We did not pursue a relationship. He deserved more, and so did I. Not everyone gets what that older couple has."

"That must not have been an easy decision. But you deserve to be loved, Eloise, and to love someone in return."

She gazed out at the sea. "Thank you. Not everyone understood, but Aunt Helena did. We agreed I should marry for love as she did, as my own parents did." She handed him her Whitby rock. "Why don't you take this back to Victoria? I think she would enjoy it very much."

Griffith put the sweet back in the paper sack and tucked it in his pocket.

Eloise stood. "I should like to keep walking."

Eloise took Griffith's arm, savoring his nearness. He was the same person she had known, and yet, he had also grown. He was more settled, more open and direct. He had a confidence about him that stemmed, she imagined, from his experiences as a businessman, as a husband, as a father. She didn't want to think about what would happen when it was time for him to leave Whitby. For now, she would enjoy the evening.

Two women rushed over to them.

"Mr. Hastings! How wonderful it is to run into you. We were just saying that we hoped to see you again. And we hope our acquaintance will continue once we are all back in London."

Eloise took her hand from Griffith's arm and stepped back. She did not recognize either of the women. One was older than the other. About the age of Mrs. Hastings. The younger woman was quite attractive, her blond hair meticulously coiffed beneath her delicate hat.

The younger woman knew how to tilt her head. How to look up from beneath her eyelashes to attract a gentleman's attention. Eloise had tried to learn the skill in London but had never mastered it.

"Mrs. Northrup, Miss Northrup, this is Miss Deighton." Griffith reached for her arm and guided her forward as if he were proud to be seen with her.

Eloise exchanged pleasantries with the ladies.

"Are you from London also?" Miss Northrup asked.

"I was there for a time, but now I reside in Whitby," Eloise said.

"Oh dear, then we shall not be able to see you when we return home," Mrs. Northrup said. Eloise was sure the woman was completely insincere. It was obvious that she was happy Eloise would not be in competition for Griffith in London.

"If you'll excuse me," Eloise said. "It's lovely to meet you, but I should really be getting home."

Griffith looked surprised. "Don't go, Miss Deighton. Not yet." He turned to the Northrups. "Are you returning to London soon?"

"On Saturday," Miss Northrup said. "We have enjoyed our time here, but we cannot extend our stay. We would love to dine with you before we leave."

Griffith was quick with his response. Tipping his hat, he said, "I regret that I will be unable to meet with you again while you are here." He offered his arm to Eloise once again. "I am already obligated elsewhere."

The women were soon on their way, and Eloise accompanied Griffith to the end of the promenade, unable to keep a smile from her lips. They stopped where the beach curved and ended in a rock formation, jutting out into the sea. Just beyond the rocks was the hidden cove where she and Griffith spent so many mornings.

"Miss Northrup was quite lovely," Eloise said.

"Was she? I hadn't noticed. I suppose she is nice enough."

"I believe your mother would approve of her."

He snorted. "She would indeed. She introduced us. But I don't need her approval. Not anymore."

He seemed distracted and Eloise followed his gaze to the rocks. He turned to her. "Do you still swim?"

She hesitated before answering him. "No. I left those things behind when I went to London."

"I have not been in the water once since coming back here. I am afraid I don't even remember how to swim." His voice was soft. Wistful.

"I don't think it is something you forget," Eloise said. "Perhaps Miss Northrup would like to swim." Now that he had made it clear he had no interest in Miss Northrup, she couldn't resist teasing him.

Griffith laughed. "Miss Northrup? Hardly. She is afraid of the fish." His face grew serious. "But there is someone who is desperate for a swim."

Her heart picked up speed. Did he guess how much she missed being in the water? If he asked her to meet him in the cove in the wee hours of the morning, she would be sorely tempted to go. An ache rose from her feet up through her entire being. The sea called her. As a lady, she had sworn off swimming, and when she first came back to Whitby, she'd been able to keep that promise to herself. But now things were different. Being with Griffith awakened within her all of the things she loved about living here and all the times she had shared with him.

Her lips were dry, and she ran her tongue over them. "Who?"

She fully anticipated him saying that he was the one desperate to swim with her. And if he asked her, she would sneak out of the house and meet him as she had so many times before.

"Victoria."

Victoria? His six-year-old daughter wanted to swim? She did not want to be responsible for Victoria in the open water. "I won't swim with her in the cove," Eloise said.

"Victoria wishes to swim in Whitby as Queen Victoria swims at Osborne Bay. She pesters me every day about using a bathing machine. She is too young to go alone, and my mother will have none of it. I would take her myself if it were allowed. If I might be so bold, would you consider taking her? I know it isn't real swimming, but it would make her very happy."

Venturing out in a bathing machine with Victoria was a completely different matter than swimming in the cove. Helping Victoria in the shallow water off the back of a cart would not be difficult, and the woman who attended the bathing cart and served as the dipper would be nearby to assist if any problems arose.

Still, she hesitated. Overhearing Victoria say she didn't want a new mother still niggled in the back of her mind. She was already fond of Victoria, and she had never stopped loving Griffith. What would happen if Victoria told Griffith she didn't want him to see Eloise anymore?

"Victoria has come back to life here in Whitby. She has color in her cheeks, and she's found her smile. Perhaps I am too indulgent of her wishes, but I would like to grant her this one thing. I know it is a lot to ask of you, and I understand completely if you say no."

Eloise faced him. While his words indicated she did not have to swim, there was no denying the pleading in his eyes. Did he know that she could never resist him?

"I will take her swimming."

He smiled wide and his cheek puckered a bit near his scar, but she didn't mind it. To her, he was as handsome as ever. Handsome, and here for now. But eventually he would leave, and she needed to prepare for that. "Griffith, I will understand if you wish to meet with Miss Northrup when you return to London. I will take Victoria swimming whether you wish to spend more time with me or not."

He dropped his gaze to her gloved hand as he entwined his fingers with hers. "I don't care to meet with Miss Northrup again. Don't you see, Eloise? In my heart, there has only ever been you."

Eloise trembled, wanting desperately to believe him. "What about Rebecca?"

She hated that she was jealous of a deceased woman, but she couldn't help it. Rebecca had married him. Had his child.

He straightened with a sigh, but he did not let go of her hand. "I did love Rebecca. She was steady, and supportive, and a good mother. But you were my first love, Eloise. I don't know how else to explain it. There is a piece of my heart that will forever belong only to you. It has been that way since the day we met."

She grimaced. "I doubt that. We were too young to be in love."

Griffith shook his head. "If you insist that we were not in love, you must at least allow that it was deep admiration. You are unlike anyone I have ever known. I never would have jumped off rocks into the sea or dived beneath the water to search for shells if it had not been for you. I like who I am when I am with you."

Eloise stared out over the water. She did not trust herself to speak. This was not the first time Griffith told her he loved her for who she was. He had always seen something in her that no one else did. She had no idea what would happen when it was time for him to go back to London. She couldn't bear to think about it.

Gripping his hand, she pulled him out onto the sand over to a large rock. He resisted, but only for a moment.

"What are you doing?" he asked.

"What I should have done here all along." She perched on the rock and took off her gloves, shoes, and stockings. Holding up her skirt, she said, "Race you," and dashed toward the water.

Griffith shed his shoes and socks and ran after her. He caught up with her by the water's edge. A wave lapped up on the shore and he gasped as the cold water washed over his feet. Eloise laughed.

"There you are, the Eloise I remember." He picked her up and spun her around before setting her back on the sand. When he bent to kiss her, her hat was in the way. She unpinned it and tossed it up on the beach where the incoming water could not reach it.

"I guess you can take the girl out of Whitby, but not take Whitby out of the girl," she said.

"Thank goodness for that." He kissed her soundly, and Eloise did not care who on the promenade might see them. She encircled his neck with her arms, pulling him close. It was perfect. The sun lowering in the sky sent golden rays across the beach. She was home. By the sea that she loved, with the man that she loved.

"When are we taking Victoria swimming?" she asked.

"Could we go tomorrow?"

She nodded, and he kissed her again. Griffith took her hand and led her back up the beach, picking up her hat from the sand. "She adores you, you know. And so do I."

CHAPTER 18

When Griffith returned to the inn, he was tired and a bit cold. Back in his room, he stripped down to his shirt and pants. He peeled off his socks and brushed the last bit of sand off his feet. When he lay back on the bed, he replayed the evening in his mind. Dancing with Eloise, eating ice cream, running across the sand after her, taking her in his arms, and giving her a kiss—it was all nothing short of magical. He couldn't remember the last time he felt so alive.

A knock at the door broke his reverie. Victoria was waiting outside his room.

"Did you see Elo…Miss Deighton?"

He ruffled her hair. "Yes, I did. And she has agreed to take you swimming."

Mrs. Hastings appeared behind her granddaughter. "I don't approve, Griffith."

He sighed. "I am sorry that you don't. You have helped me and Victoria through a very difficult time, and I will be forever grateful for that. But I must make my own decisions concerning her now. She wants to swim, and I want her to have that experience. I assure you that Miss Deighton will take very good care of her."

He bent to give Victoria a hug. "You need to get to bed so you will be well-rested for tomorrow. I would like to talk to your grandmama. She'll join you in a little while."

"Goodnight, Papa." Victoria went across the hall to her room and closed the door.

Griffith stepped aside so Mother could enter his room. She sat on the chair in the corner and clasped her hands on her lap. Her back was ramrod straight. "I believe you are spending far too much time with Miss Deighton," she said.

"You are entitled to your opinion, Mother. But you must know that I believe I have not spent nearly enough time with her. We have much to catch up on. For instance, I did not know that the two of you met before. You had a conversation with her before we left Whitby ten years ago."

Mother's eyes widened. "I have no idea what you are talking about."

"It is my understanding that you asked her to stay away from me. And I never received the letters that she wrote to me. Is it true, Mother? Did you tell Eloise not to have any more contact with me? Did you take her letters?"

"Miss Deighton was a wild thing when you met her, Griffith. If you had married her and brought her to London, you both would have been miserable. This place is a part of her. She belongs here, and you do not. It is that simple. I did what I needed to do," Mrs. Hastings said.

Before he could answer, she rose from the chair and returned to her room. Griffith was tempted to follow her, to make her apologize, but he didn't wish to disturb Victoria. Eloise was right. They could not rewrite the past. But he could choose his future.

MOTHER DID NOT JOIN him and Victoria for breakfast, claiming she did not feel well.

"We shall have to entertain ourselves this morning," he said to Victoria.

"When are we going swimming?" she asked.

"We aren't meeting Miss Deighton until afternoon, when it will be warmer. I have something to show you."

Together he and Victoria walked to a view of the coast. Two twenty-foot whale bones stood erect, forming an arch. He stopped and showed her how, when they stood in the right place, they could see the ruins of Whitby Abbey off in the distance, framed by the whale bones.

"What are they?" Victoria asked.

"Bones from a whale. Whaling ships used to sail from here, and when they returned after a hunt, they hung a whalebone from the mast to let everyone know they were safe. They don't hunt whales anymore, but the arch is here as a reminder."

Victoria touched one of the whale bones and stood beneath the arch, staring up at the top.

"Lift me up," she said.

Griffith hoisted her to his shoulders. She stretched out her arms, reaching as high up the whalebone as she could.

"I can't reach the top," she said.

Griffith set her back down. "No, it's at least three times as tall as me."

He took her hand, and they walked back toward the inn. The sea was calm in the distance.

"Will there be whales when we go swimming?"

"No, they don't come that close to shore."

"Have you ever seen a whale?"

"Once," he said. "It was likely a minke whale." He'd been thrilled to see the spray off in the distance. Eloise had not been as excited. "They eat the mackerel," she'd said. "And the herring."

Griffith pointed toward the horizon. "If you watch way out there, you might see a whale blow."

He and Victoria gazed at the horizon for a long time, but they did not spot a whale.

"I'd like to see one someday," Victoria said. "I like it here, Papa."

"Me, too. Tell me, what do you think of Miss Deighton?"

"She's my friend," Victoria said. "Why doesn't Grandmama like her?"

He paused, wondering what was appropriate to tell Victoria. "Maybe she doesn't know Miss Deighton as well as we do yet."

Satisfied, Victoria skipped down the path as they headed back to the inn.

MOTHER MET THEM FOR LUNCH. When the food arrived, Victoria turned up her nose.

"I would like bread and jam," she said. "Or Yorkshire pudding."

"You'll have to wait until dinner for Yorkshire pudding, but I'll ask someone to bring you bread and jam," Griffith said.

He waved the waitress over and made the request. When the woman returned with bread and jam, Victoria reached for it, but Mother stopped her.

"Eat your other food first, Victoria," Mother said. "You shouldn't indulge her, Griffith."

"It won't hurt her to eat whatever she wants this one time," he said.

Victoria slathered jam on a thick slice of bread and took a bite. Jam dribbled down her chin.

"Use your napkin!" Mrs. Hastings said.

"She is all right, Mother. Let her be."

"She must learn to mind her manners!" Mrs. Hastings took her own napkin to wipe Victoria's chin. Griffith stopped her.

"Victoria has plenty of time to learn how to be proper. I want her to learn that it never hurts to ask for what she wants. She may not get it, but it is fine to ask. And I want her to learn that we should take pleasure in life. It isn't all rules and manners. Those things have their place but so does a layer of jam so thick that it slides down your face."

Victoria grinned. "Are you coming to watch me swim, Grandmama?"

Mother set her napkin on the table. "I am sure you don't need me. I will be grateful when we return to London."

Griffith sighed. "We do need you, Mother, and you are welcome to come with us."

"Please," Victoria said. "I want you to see me in the water. And then you can get to know Eloise."

Mrs. Hastings raised an eyebrow at Griffith.

He shrugged. "There is much to appreciate about Miss Deighton. I would like you to get to know her a little more before you make up your mind about her."

Mrs. Hastings carefully placed her knife and fork across her plate. Her actions were slow and deliberate. "Miss Deighton seems more…refined, more mature than she used to be. If this is what you want, I shall try."

"Thank you, Mother," he said. He stood up as she rose from the table.

"I only ever wanted what is best for you," she said.

"I know that. And now I want what is best for Victoria, and for me."

It was all he could ask for. Mother was fair-minded, and in time, he hoped both she and Eloise would reach an understanding.

CHAPTER 19

*E*loise hurried downstairs, her long hair braided for swimming. She hoped to slip away unnoticed. Johnny and Thomas were busily playing, but Mary was seated nearby feeding the baby. "Going somewhere?" she asked.

"I am going to the beach. I promised Mr. Hastings I would accompany his daughter in a bathing machine."

Father came out of the kitchen. "He asked you to take his daughter swimming, did he?"

Eloise nodded.

Father grinned at her. "He must want you to connect with his little girl. He's seeing if the three of you are a match."

Although she didn't want to admit it, she had a very similar thought. Her cheeks burned, and she knew they were flushing bright pink.

"Father! I am only doing it as a favor. You know he cannot take his daughter in a bathing machine himself."

"Have you decided that this is what you want? This man and his child?" Father asked.

Eloise was aware of Mary's eyes on her as she considered

the question. Spending time with Griffith filled a void within her that nothing else touched. Parts of herself that she had pushed aside or tried hard to forget resurfaced when she was around him. Because of that, she now understood that the only way she would truly be at home in Whitby was to be herself completely. Both the London version of herself and the Whitby part of herself. They had to coexist in order for her to be whole.

Her family would never understand her London side. But Griffith did. And now that she had lived in London, she understood that part of him as she never had before.

"I am not certain, Father, but I must find out. No matter how it ends, I want to see it through."

He walked over to her and grasped her hands. "I will support you no matter what you decide. Tell Mr. Hastings I said hello."

"Thank you, Father," Eloise said. She kissed his grizzled cheek and hurried out the door.

Eloise headed to the beach with a spring in her step. White clouds drifted lazily in the sky and the sun was warm on her face. It was the perfect afternoon for a swim.

She arrived at the bathing machines with her stomach swirling like darting fish. Losing Griffith once drove her from her beloved sea, and now it seemed only fitting that being reunited with him again would bring her back to the water. She shaded her eyes and scanned the promenade, searching for him. Her heart leapt when she spotted him.

He made eye contact and came toward her. She watched him approach, tall and lean, so familiar and so dear. Victoria was by his side.

"Eloise!" Victoria reached her first and gave her a big hug. "Are you ready to swim?"

"Yes, I am," Eloise said, returning the hug. She was surprised how much she had come to care for Victoria in such a short time. Father was right. This outing was a chance for them to see if they could become a family. The realization made her suddenly awkward around Griffith, not knowing what to say to him. Did the gravity of the situation bother him as well?

His eyes were filled with warmth as he smiled at her. "Victoria hasn't given me a moment's peace. She's been very eager for this all morning. I have a plan. See the demarcation between the men's side and the women's side? I shall choose a bathing machine near the divide, and you two shall be in a bathing machine on the other side. Then we shall be able to see each other."

"And should you drift across the line, you might end up swimming with your daughter," Eloise said, meeting his eyes.

"You and I would never bend the rules like that," Griffith said, winking at her.

She smiled at his words. His ease in their situation helped her to relax and she was determined to enjoy the afternoon.

When they reached the bathing machines, Griffith engaged two carts for them.

"See you soon," he said. He kissed Victoria's head. "Listen to Miss Deighton."

Victoria grabbed Eloise's hand and tugged. Eloise laughed and followed her to the bathing machine.

Once inside, they changed into their swimming attire. Eloise let the attendant know they were ready. She sat with Victoria as the horse pulled the cart into the water. It lurched sideways once on the uneven sand, and Victoria gasped.

"What happens if we tip over?"

"I would help you. But I don't think you need to worry." Sure enough, the cart straightened and the slow ride into the water continued

"Are you afraid?" Eloise asked.

"A little," Victoria said, suddenly solemn.

"The water will be a bit cold," Eloise said. "It's best to get wet quickly. The dipper can help you if you would like."

"What if I wash away?" Victoria asked.

Eloise squeezed her hand. "You won't. We won't be in deep water, and the waves are calm today. It's the perfect day for your first swim."

"Is it your first swim?"

Eloise shook her head. "No. I used to help my father sometimes with his fishing boat, and I learned to swim when I was about your age."

The bathing machine stopped, and Eloise opened the door, guiding Victoria out onto the little platform.

"You go first," Victoria said.

Eloise stepped into the water and gasped at the cold. Her feet sank slightly in the sandy bottom, and the water swirled around her thighs. It was better than she imagined, being back in the sea. She tipped her face toward the sun and closed her eyes, relishing the feeling. It had been too long.

She turned to Victoria and held out her hands. "Come on. You will be fine."

Victoria hesitated. She gripped Eloise's hands and jumped into the water with a splash. Eloise crouched until she was eye level with Victoria. "If you lie on your back, the water will hold you up."

"No," Victoria said, shaking her head. "I'll drown."

"I won't let anything happen to you." She put one arm behind Victoria's neck and the other behind her back and coaxed her to lie back into the water.

"Don't let go of me."

"I'll stay right here. But the water will hold you." Eloise slowly lowered her arms.

Victoria stayed afloat for a moment until she realized she was no longer being supported. She sat up and caught a wave in her face. Sputtering, she floundered in the water, splashing her arms in panic.

"Stand up," Eloise said, grasping her arm. Victoria set her feet down. The water was below her shoulders.

"See? Everything is all right," Eloise assured her. She steadied Victoria as gentle waves rolled in, lifting and lowering them.

"Do you trust me?" Eloise asked.

Victoria solemnly nodded her head.

"Keep your head up out of the water and lay on your stomach. I'll hold you up, and you can pull with your arms and kick with your legs," Eloise said.

Victoria complied and soon was happily moving her arms and legs as Eloise carried her through the water. "Where's Papa?" she asked.

Eloise spied a head bobbing toward them. "I see him," she said, changing direction so they could join him.

"I'm swimming!" Victoria announced in triumph.

"Yes, you are," Griffith said, his face lighting up with a smile.

Eloise moved Victoria closer to Griffith and the child flung her arms around her father's neck. He held her tight, spinning around and around. Victoria laughed and splashed.

"Stand up, Papa! Lift me up high!"

Griffith shook his head. "Not today. I'm not supposed to be over here on the women's side. We have to be very stealthy, so I don't get caught."

With Victoria occupied, Eloise lay on her back and stared up at the clouds. The water cradled her, welcoming her back. She closed her eyes, letting herself drift.

"Miss! Miss, don't go too far!"

Eloise lifted her head and saw the attendant waving frantically at her. Not wanting to cause the woman any distress, she took a breath and swam back toward the bathing cart.

When she lifted her head, the dipper grinned at her. "I thought you were one of those fancy tourists who'd never been in the sea, but you know how to swim."

"I grew up here," Eloise said.

"Go on then. Let me know when you are ready to get out."

Eloise swam lazily back over to Griffith and Victoria.

Let's look for shells," Griffith said. He knelt on the sand and showed Victoria how to hold her breath and peer under the water.

"The salt burns my eyes."

"Only for a minute." Griffith held up a shell. "See if you can find one."

When Victoria ducked under the surface, he smiled at Eloise. "Enjoying yourself?"

"Very much. Victoria is a natural. She'll be swimming in no time."

Victoria stood up, raising her fist. "Look at my shell!"

It was a small shell, scallop shaped, and striped. "It's perfect," Griffith said. "Today is perfect. Thank you, Eloise. You've made us both very happy."

He held her gaze as a wave nudged her gently toward him. Eloise wanted to be close to him, have him wrap his arms around her, feel his warmth. "You've made me very happy, too."

The three of them splashed and looked for shells until Victoria's teeth were chattering from the cold water. Griffith said goodbye and swam back over to his bathing machine. Eloise wondered briefly if he had paid his attendant to look the other way when he left the men's area. But she was grateful that he had.

Back inside the bathing machine, Eloise helped Victoria towel off and change into dry clothes. The cart rocked gently as it carried them back to shore. Water dripped from Eloise's braid onto her dress. She'd have to rinse the salt water out of her hair when she got home, but she didn't mind.

When the cart stopped, Griffith was waiting for them on the beach. Eloise didn't bother to put her shoes on as they crossed the sand.

"Can we go again, Papa?" Victoria asked.

"I hope so, but we cannot take up all of Miss Deighton's afternoons."

"But Eloise loves the water, don't you?"

"Yes, I do. And I loved being in the water with you." She met Griffith's eyes. It was so right to be here with them. To share the sea and her love of water with Victoria as she had shared it with Griffith.

Victoria walked between them. She took their hands and swung their arms. Eloise didn't want the afternoon to end. This was more than she ever imagined. Griffith and Victoria felt like her family.

A tall, straight-backed figure carrying a parasol stood on the promenade watching them. Before they reached her, the woman walked away. Eloise glanced at Griffith, but he hadn't noticed. She was certain it was Mrs. Hastings, and she wondered what the woman would say about her being with Griffith and Victoria at the beach.

It was with some surprise that Eloise realized that it no longer mattered to her what Mrs. Hastings thought. What mattered was the time she'd shared with Victoria and Griffith. No one could take today away from her.

Back on the promenade, they sat on a bench and put on their socks and shoes. Griffith helped Victoria with one shoe while Eloise helped with the other. Their hands brushed while they fastened her shoes.

"I wish it could always be like this," Victoria said.

Me, too, Eloise thought. *Me, too.*

CHAPTER 20

When Griffith returned to the inn, he found a letter from Robert awaiting him. He read it quickly, frown lines creasing his forehead. There was no getting around it. He would have to return to London immediately. Robert needed his assistance with a supplier who was in breach of a merchandising agreement. Since Griffith had brokered the deal, the man would not negotiate with anyone else. He must cut their trip short and take Mother and Victoria back home with him. But he had things he wanted to discuss with Eloise.

He delivered Victoria to his mother before hurrying to his own room. He found paper, a pen, and ink.

Dear Eloise,

Business calls me away, and I must return to London. I will take the first train out tomorrow. But there are things I need to discuss with you before I leave. Please meet me tonight at sundown. I'll be waiting on the bench where I found you with Victoria. If you are not able to meet, send me a message at the inn.

Griffith

He hesitated, the pen hovering over the page. He moved it

in time to prevent a drop of ink from splotching the paper and making a mess of things. This was his third draft of the note.

If anyone else read the letter, they would be shocked both by the term of endearment and also his use of their given names. But he and Eloise had started their friendship as Eloise and Griffith. And no matter what happened moving forward, he wanted it to be that way between them, not Miss Deighton and Mr. Hastings. He liked to think that underneath all the changes, all the years that had gone by, they were still simply two people who met in the sea and fell in love.

He folded the note, sealed it with wax, and wrote her name on the outside. He'd have someone from the inn deliver it to her. She had to meet him. She would, wouldn't she? He was not aware of anything that would stand in their way.

He carried the letter downstairs and found one of the young men who worked at the inn.

"I need you to deliver this to Miss Deighton immediately. Do you know her?"

"Matthew Deighton's daughter? I know the house. I'll take it right away."

Griffith handed him the letter. He reminded himself that it was not scandalous to send a note, so why were his nerves rattling his ribs as if he were doing something wrong? He and Eloise had been very open about their friendship, even strolling along the promenade together. All of Whitby must know of their interactions by now.

He headed back to his room and met Victoria and his mother.

"You are not ready for dinner. Were you going somewhere? Or coming back?" Mother asked.

"Neither. I had to send a message."

"What was so urgent?"

"Robert needs my assistance, and we must return to London tomorrow morning. I have sent a message to Miss Deighton asking if I might meet with her tonight," Griffith said.

"Has something happened to Robert?" Mrs. Hastings asked.

"He's well, Mother. It is a business negotiation gone awry, but it needs my immediate attention."

Relief washed over Mother's face. "I am glad Robert is well. I shall help Victoria pack after we've eaten."

Victoria tugged on his hand. "We have to go home? Will we be coming back?"

"Yes, we have to go home. I don't know when I will be able to bring you back, but I hope it won't be long."

Mrs. Hastings' lips formed a thin line, but she said nothing.

"Can I say goodbye to Eloise?"

Mrs. Hastings frowned. "May I. And you must call her Miss Deighton."

Griffith ignored his mother and focused on Victoria. "You can't come with me tonight, but I shall tell her goodbye for you. She will understand."

"Will I ever see her again?"

"I hope so," Griffith said, meeting his mother's gaze.

"I don't want to go back to London." Victoria's lower lip jutted out in a familiar pout. "I like it here. I want to find more shells and go for another swim. Eloise said she knows the names of the birds we see on the shore, and she is going to teach me."

"If all goes well, we shall both be back in Whitby very soon. But now, we must have dinner and then get everything in order for the train tomorrow."

Victoria was thrilled to have Yorkshire pudding, but even

the rich brown gravy and roast beef couldn't tempt his appetite. After the meal, he packed methodically, leaving the ammonite on the dresser until last. He regretted not reuniting his half with Eloise's yet, but it would have to wait until he returned.

GRIFFITH PERCHED on the edge of the bench, fidgeting as the sun dropped lower in the sky. While the sight of the water usually calmed him, tonight he was unable to sit still. He'd arrived early, and he kept twisting around to watch for Eloise.

At long last, he spotted her. He jumped up and went toward her, unable to wait for her to reach him. She was not wearing a hat, and he longed to unpin her hair and let it tumble down in long, loose waves. He reached for her hand, but she withdrew it from him.

"From the moment I saw you here, I knew your time in Whitby was limited. I knew you would have to leave again. But I must confess, I did not know your departure would come so soon," she said.

"I would not leave unless it was absolutely necessary. Please sit. I have things I wish to say to you." Griffith removed his hat and ran his hands over the brim, gathering his thoughts.

"Eloise," he began.

She placed her hand on his arm. "Let me say this first. Please."

He leaned back against the bench, still turning the hat over and over in his hands. "Go on, then."

"Before you say anything, you must know this," she said. "Whitby is my home. I left it once, but I won't leave it again. My heart is here, with my family. I belong here by the sea. I could never move back to London."

Griffith's hands stilled. "I would never ask you to leave. I didn't come back to Whitby to cause you any further hurt, Eloise."

"I know," she said softly. "At least this time you have come to say goodbye in person." She rose from the bench and walked away from him.

He followed her. He guessed she was walking away in order to conceal her emotions from him, but he had not yet told her what he wished to say. He caught up to her and she stopped, but she did not face him.

"At least let me tell you why I need to leave," he said.

"You don't have to explain to me. I know your life is in London, and mine is here."

"Eloise, please look at me, please listen."

She turned toward him and slowly met his gaze. Her eyes were brimming with tears. He had hurt her again, despite his best intentions not to. With all his heart, he wished to make it better.

Gently, he touched her cheek and wiped a tear. "Please don't cry, Eloise. What I have to say is not meant to cause you grief. I came back to Whitby because I was always happy here, and I wanted to be happy again. But it wasn't Whitby that made me happy."

"Then you must go where you will be happy," she said. Her lower lip trembled.

"You misunderstand me." Griffith grasped her hand and brought it to his mouth, planting a kiss on her palm. She shivered at his touch.

"It was you."

She gave him a questioning look.

"From the moment I saw you with Victoria on the promenade, I knew we belonged together. Whitby never made me happy, Eloise. But you did. All of my happy memories here are with you, and I shall be happy wherever you are. I want a future with you. I want you and me and Victoria to be a family, if you'll have us."

"But what about your business and your life in London?"

"Robert and I have discussed expanding the business. If we move forward, he will continue to run things in London, and I would open an office somewhere else. Someplace with a fishery, and jewelry, and textiles that need to be transported to London. I would have work here, Eloise, if you want me to stay."

Eloise rubbed her arms in the cool evening air. Griffith moved behind her and put his arms around her. She leaned back against him, and he kissed her hair. Was she silent because she didn't know what to say? Or because she didn't want to be with him? If it was the latter, he didn't want to hear her say it.

"Don't give me an answer tonight," he said softly. "I shall complete my business in London as quickly as possible and return to Whitby. You may give me your answer then. If you want me here, I'll be here. If you want me to go back to London and not be part of your life, I'll respect your choice."

Eloise shifted toward him and placed her hands on his chest. "I don't want you to go, but I know you must."

He pressed his forehead against hers. "And I don't want to leave. But I promise you I will come back."

"How long will you be gone?" she asked.

"Not long. No more than a week, I imagine." The waves lapped the shore while he held her.

"And Victoria?" Eloise asked.

"I will leave Victoria with Mother in London for now. If I open an office here, I'll have her join me once I am settled. Mother will stay in London, but Victoria loves the sea as much as I do. I would like to raise her here in Whitby. She says you offered to teach her the names of the birds."

Eloise smiled at that. Griffith placed his finger under her chin and tilted her face toward him. Her eyes were shining.

He bent his head down, his lips meeting hers. As her arms went around his neck, he deepened the kiss. He hoped the gentle pressure of his mouth on hers conveyed his sincerity, hoped that she would sense his reluctance to leave her.

When he released her, she stood before him with her eyes closed, quiet and vulnerable.

CHAPTER 21

$\mathcal{E}$loise allowed Griffith to accompany her down the promenade until they neared her street. "I can walk the rest of the way alone. Have a safe journey, and I'll see you soon."

"I will be counting the days until I am with you again," he said, and headed to the Seaside Inn.

She stared after him for a moment. The breeze off the water cooled her flushed cheeks. Instead of sadness looming in her mind, she felt a spark of hope. Perhaps the reason she hadn't been truly at home in Whitby after her return had nothing to do with the town or her family. Maybe it was not Whitby that was her home, but Griffith Hastings and the life they could build together.

But did she dare hope? If it were only Griffith, then she would accept him immediately. But Mrs. Hastings was still an obstacle. Despite her best efforts to prove herself worthy of the Hastings family, she was certain that Mrs. Hastings had not changed her opinion. As Eloise turned onto her street and approached her home, a woman stepped out of the shadows.

"Miss Deighton?"

Eloise jumped. She squinted at the figure in the dim light. "Mrs. Hastings?"

"I did not mean to startle you. I know you were meeting my son," she said.

"Mrs. Hastings, with all due respect, if you have come to tell me to stay away from him again, I am in no mood to listen," Eloise said. It was hard for her to hold her ground with this woman, but she was determined to stand up for herself.

"While I do not regret my words to you so many years ago, that is not my purpose in meeting you tonight. I am leaving Whitby tomorrow, and I wanted to speak to you before I left. Since I arrived here with Griffith and Victoria, I have seen a change in them. A change for the better. Victoria adores you, as does he. For better or for worse, he has made up his mind that you are the reason for his happiness, and I have seen no evidence to the contrary. I am first and foremost a mother, Miss Deighton. What I want for Griffith is for his heart to heal, for him to be happy once more. I have come to tell you that should you and Griffith decide to move forward together, I shall not stand in the way."

Eloise was speechless. She had never imagined Mrs. Hastings would reach out to her in this manner and she fumbled for something to say.

"Griffith and I have not yet made any decisions," she said. "But I do care for him and Victoria. I want them to be happy, too."

Mrs. Hastings' face was in shadow, and Eloise was unable to read her expression. Her posture was somehow softer, not as stiff as Eloise remembered her being during their previous encounters. "Victoria enjoyed her swim immensely. You took very good care of her."

"It was you I saw on the promenade," Eloise said.

Mrs. Hastings nodded. "I wanted to see all of you together for myself, without my presence altering your behavior. I…." She paused, as if it was difficult for her to force out the words she wanted to say. "It was…good to see how you are with them when no one is watching."

"Thank you, Mrs. Hastings. And please, call me Eloise."

"As you wish. Goodnight, Eloise." With that, Mrs. Hastings squared her shoulders and walked sedately down the street toward the inn.

Eloise entered the house and quietly closed the door behind her. She didn't wish to wake anyone. The children would all be in bed, and John retired early so that he might head out at dawn to fish. She leaned back against the door in wonder, replaying the evening's conversation in her head.

And Griffith. She put her hand to her mouth, remembering the tenderness of his lips when he kissed her. He had always loved her. She made her way upstairs and dressed for bed. He was offering her what she had always wanted, a life with him built on love. The days could not pass quickly enough until she could see him again and give him her answer.

By the time Eloise awakened, the children were already downstairs. Mary was feeding them breakfast while her father held the baby.

"Good morning, sleepyhead," Father said. "What happened between you and Mr. Hastings last night?"

The memory of Griffith holding her and the kiss they'd shared warmed her cheeks. "He wanted to tell me he is returning to London today on the morning train."

"Oh, Eloise! He is leaving again? Is it over between you?" Mary asked.

"He said he would return, that he wants to run a business here in Whitby. He suggested a future for us and asked me to give him an answer when he comes back." Eloise picked up a piece of bread and sat at the table.

Father grunted. "And what will your answer be, daughter? Can you picture a life with him?"

Late into the night, that was all she pictured. She imagined them at the breakfast table sharing a meal and attending church together with Victoria. She pictured them taking walks on the beach or up to the abbey ruins. He would leave for work in the morning and return home to her in the evenings. She would visit Mary and take Victoria to play with Johnny and Thomas. Warmth washed over her like a gentle wave. The happiness that evaded her for so long now filled her heart.

"It is difficult for me to picture a life without him," she said.

"Do you have an understanding?" Father asked.

"Not formally. He would like my answer when he returns."

"But you know what your answer is?"

"Yes, Father."

"Then why are you here? You must tell him. Why wait for him to return?"

"It's not that simple," Eloise said.

"Men are very simple creatures, Eloise. If he wants your answer, he is ready for it now. His only concern is that you are not yet ready."

"He is getting on the train," she said. "It shall have to wait."

"Not if you hurry," Father said. "When you know what you want, you must go after it with your whole heart. That's what I did with your mother."

Father was right. Why should she wait, hoping that Griffith would return? It would be better to give him a solid reason to come back. She did not bother to put on her hat as she burst out the door. A lady would walk, but the girl who ran barefoot through Whitby had other ideas. Eloise broke into a run.

She arrived at the train station out of breath as the whistle blew and the train pulled away. She stood alone on the platform, panting. The engine left behind a plume of steam as her heart sunk to her knees. She walked slowly home.

Griffith was gone. She had not told him what was in her heart. Now she must wait and hope that he would return, and that when he did, his feelings would be unchanged.

LATE THAT AFTERNOON, Eloise took Johnny and Thomas to the beach so that Mary and the baby could rest. She spread a blanket out on the sand. Thomas immediately settled down to dig a hole, while Johnny searched for shells. Each time he found one, he ran to show it to Eloise. Before long, a small collection rested in a row on the blanket's edge.

"Choose your favorite to take home and let's leave the rest for someone else to find," Eloise said.

Johnny spent several minutes sorting through the shells. He picked up two, compared them, discarded one, and started the process all over again.

"This one is for you." Johnny held up a pale pink shell.

"It's beautiful," Eloise said. "Thank you."

She tucked the shell in her handbag. She shook out the blanket, folded it, and took Thomas' hand. Johnny walked alongside Thomas. As they passed the sea wall, Eloise glanced at the niche. She expected it to be empty, but to her surprise, a familiar white shell rested inside.

Eloise told Johnny to take Thomas inside the sweet shop.

"You may each choose one treat. I shall be inside in a moment."

Her hands trembled as she pulled the pink shell out of her bag. Someone must have discovered their hiding place. Griffith could not have left the shell. He was gone.

Hands trembling, Eloise took the white shell and left the pink one in its place. Even though he was not in Whitby, even though no one else would know the significance of her message, Eloise knew that she would be at the beach early in the morning, waiting as she used to for Griffith to come.

THE SKY WAS FAINTLY PINK as Eloise shivered on her favorite rock on the beach. She was dressed in her swimming outfit, long tunic over knee-length bloomers. Stockings covered her lower legs. Her head was bare; her hair bound in a single braid.

The gray water gave way to frothy waves that bubbled onto the sand. The sea seemed to whisper her name. Griffith would not come. She knew that. But even if he did not come, she planned to float in the swells as she used to do. She had been away too long, and it was time to be herself again.

One more minute. She would wait for him one more minute. Seabirds flew over the water, and she scanned the horizon for a whale or dolphin but saw nothing. The minute went by. And then two. Soon Whitby would awaken, and it would be too late for her to swim.

Hands closed over her eyes, and she jumped as a voice called out, "Boo!"

She pulled the hands from her face as she rose from the rock.

"Griffith! I saw the train leaving. How are you here?"

"I got on the train, but I couldn't do it, Eloise. I could not leave you again. I got off at the first stop and caught the next train back here. I didn't know if you would come today. I hoped you would. Will you swim with me?" He held out his hand and she took it.

This was it. They were together again in the place where it all started. Eloise wanted to pinch herself to make sure it was real. Griffith had come back for her. She squeezed his hand. "Ready?"

They ran, hand in hand, into the waves. The cold water took her breath away, but she continued on until the water was up to her waist.

Griffith pulled her close, holding her in his arms as the incoming waves rocked them.

"If we get all the way wet, it will be warmer," he said.

"I suspect a very wise woman told you that once."

He grinned at her. "Yes. Race you to the rocks?"

She took off first, pulling hard with her arms and kicking her feet, and Griffith followed. Before they reached the rocks, she stopped and flipped on her back, floating and looking up at the sky. The swells lifted her gently. If she'd known it would feel this good to be back in the sea, she would have come to the water long ago. It was as if she'd never left.

He took her hand, and his warmth flowed through her. It was familiar and safe to be here with him.

The sun rose higher in the sky, and she knew they wouldn't be alone much longer. "We need to get back to shore," she said. She swam inland until her feet touched the sand. Griffith stood beside her.

"Thank you for bringing me back to the sea," she said.

"You brought me back to life. Thank you for healing my heart," he said.

Her fingers traced the scar on his cheek and touched his

lips. "I went to the train station to find you. I wanted to tell you that I didn't need more time to decide."

Griffith held her close. "It has been too long since we have been like this. I have a question to ask you."

She shivered. "I'm ready."

"Are you sure?"

She frowned at him. "Is that your question?"

Griffith kissed her forehead. "No. My question is this. Eloise Deighton, will you be my wife?"

Eloise searched his face, his beloved, scarred face. His green eyes held her gaze and time stood still. She was unaware of anything except Griffith. She nestled closer, drawing warmth from his touch.

"Your mother came to see me."

His jaw tensed. "And?"

"She said she would not stand in our way. But what about Victoria? I heard her say once how she did not want another mother."

"She doesn't want just any mother. She wants you."

He bent his head toward her and kissed her neck. As his lips trailed up toward her face, she trembled in anticipation. Once long ago, Griffith had nearly kissed her in the sea, and she could hardly wait for him to kiss her now.

Griffith tucked a stray strand of hair behind her ear with one hand, his other arm holding her tight. They bobbed in the water and he kissed her cheek.

"Do you have an answer? Will you be my bride?"

She gazed at his lips. Wet. Inviting. "Yes, Griffith, I will marry you. A thousand times yes."

She met his lips with her own in a kiss filled with longing and heartache and hope and healing. He tasted salty and the warmth of his kiss traveled down her spine to her toes. Kissing him in the sea was even better than she'd imagined.

She tangled her fingers in his hair as he kissed her again and again.

"We need to go," he said softly. Whitby was waking. "You need to get home before we are caught."

Reluctantly, she swam with him to the shore. When they reached the beach, he wrapped her in a blanket, and she clung to him. Her cold hands trembled as she found his lips once again.

"I'll come to your house later and speak to your father."

She wrung water from her braid and clothes. As they walked to her street, he held her hand. She never wanted to unlace her fingers from his.

"Griffith, do you love me?"

"Have I not told you?" he asked.

"Yes, but I'd like to hear it again."

He stopped and pressed his forehead against hers, drawing her into his arms. "I love you, Eloise Deighton. I always have. I always will. I cannot wait to prove it to you every day for the rest of our lives."

EPILOGUE

*E*loise and Griffith held hands as they walked out of St. Mary's church as husband and wife. Tradition dictated that they should look neither to the left or the right as they left the church, but when Eloise sneaked a peek at Griffith, he was looking at her. The smile on her face was radiant.

Victoria, who had acted as a flower girl, waited with her grandmother for their turn to exit. Eloise's father followed the couple out of the church while Griffith's brother remained behind to pay the clergyman.

It was all very traditional. Eloise wore white with a long train and veil. Griffith had gifted her a simple tiara that held the veil in place. The gold band on her finger was engraved with their initials and the wedding date.

The party that followed at the Deighton residence was simple. The cakes were cut, the guests were served. That afternoon, Eloise and Griffith boarded the train that would take them on their honeymoon trip.

"I have a gift for you, wife," Griffith said, rummaging in a valise.

She furrowed her brow. "I did not get you anything."

He pulled out one half of an ammonite fossil. "Our hearts are united now, and I think our fossils should be reunited as well."

Eloise took it from him with a grin. She reached into her handbag and pulled out her half. "I have brought mine also. You are right, husband, it is time that they were reunited."

They fit the pieces of ammonite together, and Griffith tucked the fossils back into his bag. Eloise rested her head on his shoulder.

"I shall miss Victoria while we are away," she murmured.

"I shall miss her, too. But we won't be away long. She will return to London with Robert and Mother, and we will collect her on our way back to Whitby. She is very excited to have cousins."

"Johnny and Thomas are excited as well."

Eloise took Griffith's hand and rested it on her lap. She traced each one of his fingers and the lines in his palm.

"Do you want more children?" she asked.

He closed his hand around hers. "I do. Especially if they have your eyes. Do you?"

"Yes, a houseful."

They sat together, holding hands, as the scenery raced by. "And we shall teach them all to swim," Eloise said.

"To swim, to find fossils, to catch fish, to explore the ruins by moonlight. And we shall tell them the story of how the sea brought us together," Griffith said.

Eloise grinned as she squeezed his hand. She never dreamed as a girl of twelve that the boy she met one summer day in the sea would be her husband. It had taken them years to reach this place, but now, she wanted to savor every day.

"When we get back to Whitby, we must go for a swim."

"Early, just the two of us," Griffith agreed.

Wherever their lives took them, Eloise knew that she and Griffith would always return to the sea.

"I love you, Eloise Hastings," Griffith said.

"I love you too," she said. And as he leaned over and kissed her, she knew that with Griffith, she was finally home.

The End

AUTHOR'S NOTE

Dear Reader,

A picture is worth a thousand words! When I first signed on to participate in the Victorians at the Beach series, I was a little intimidated by the Victorian Era. After all, it extends from 1837 to 1903. Where to begin? Early in the project, before I even had a draft written, I needed to choose an image for the book cover. I loved the dress style you see on the cover, and that helped me figure out details of the story. Dress styles changed quite a bit during the era, so I narrowed my time period in part, based on my cover image. I was also able to incorporate the blue dress into my story. I hope in this case, that if you do judge this book by the cover, that you love it as much as I do!

The summer beach theme of the series led me to explore seaside resort towns in England, and I have not even scratched the surface of all that Whitby, England has to offer. From the jet jewelry (popularized when Queen Victoria wore a piece of it to mourn Prince Albert), to the Whitby Abbey ruins that inspired Bram Stoker when he was writing Dracula, there is so much to explore in this wonderful place. Whitby has a history of whaling, smugglers, explorers (Captain Cook), and I hope to revisit this setting in future books.

Thank you for reading this novella! Griffith and Eloise ended up being two of my favorite characters (as well as Victoria), and I hope you loved them, too. I am so grateful for readers who make this writing journey possible,

If you'd like to connect, you can follow me on social media or contact me/subscribe to my newsletter on my website www.amynewbold.com.

Happy reading!

Amy

ACKNOWLEDGMENTS

I am honored to participate in this multi-author project with the following talented writers: Jill E. Warner, Sienna Peake, Heloise C. Kensington, and Karen M. Edwards. If you have not already done so, consider reading their wonderful books!

A special thank you to Madisyn at Mountain Peak Edits and Design for her beautiful book covers.

It takes a village to create a book. I am blessed to have an incredibly supportive team.

First and foremost, huge thanks to my family: **Greg, Josie, Daniel, Shannon, Will, Maren, Joan, Jodean, and Claris**. Shout out to Josie who, when I was stuck, helped me get Griffith and Eloise on the promenade. When the writing gets tough, it is all of you who keep me going.

A special thanks to my beta readers: Greg, Daniel, Lark, Karen, and Celeste. This story is so much better because of the feedback you gave. I particularly appreciate Greg and Lark for their patience in reading multiple versions of this story. Both Eloise and Griffith are stronger characters because of your thoughtful insights. Karen helped make this story more authentic to the UK setting and any remaining errors are mine.

And finally, thank you to my readers! Without you, I would be writing in a void. I am so grateful that you share in this journey.

Amy Newbold enjoys writing sweet, clean romances, and the occasional ghost story. She learned to read at age four and has been reading and writing ever since. Her favorite thing about writing romance is capturing that first spark of falling in love and sharing it on the written page. Amy loves traveling, playing board games, being in nature, and spending time with her family. She has a deep appreciation for chocolate and is living her own happily-ever-after with her husband, illustrator Greg Newbold.

To receive writing updates, learn about new releases, have access to special sales, get book recommendations, and more, subscribe to Amy's newsletter on her website: https://www.amynewbold.com

ALSO BY AMY NEWBOLD

Sweet & Clean Romance:

A Lady Most Alluring: A Grimm Regency Tale

Picture Books:

If Picasso Painted a Snowman

If Da Vinci Painted a Dinosaur

If Monet Painted a Monster

For an updated list of Amy's books, please visit her website: https://
www.amynewbold.com

GET SWEPT AWAY WITH A VICTORIAN SEASIDE ROMANCE

Between Shores and Scandals by Jill E. Warner

Clara Ward has dreamed of returning to Margate ever since her grandmother brought her as a little girl. Now, after years of working toward buying her own home and starting a gourmet ices shop, Clara's goals are finally within reach. When a startling encounter with local doctor Ellis Archibald threatens to create a scandal before Clara has a chance to even start work, the enigmatic doctor proposes a marriage of convenience.

Between family and friends' expectations, preparing her shop for its grand opening, and rescuing her own reputation, Clara feels the pressure of convincing everyone that she married for love. As she falls for Ellis on the shores of Margate's beaches, Clara must decide whether her reputation and her shop's future is worth upholding the lies or if the truth is worth causing a greater scandal.

Of Fossils and Follies by Sienna Peake

Will an unexpected summer yield more than one discovery?

Ever since she was a young girl studying geology with her father, Opal Martin has longed for the chance to visit Lyme Regis and dig for discoveries of her own. When a high-stakes contest partners her with the stiff and grumpy Mr. Harris, Opal hardly expects to find love along her quest for fossils.

Nigel Harris has had to work his way up from humble origins to become an assistant to the famous geologist, Gideon Buckston. The last thing he needs is a pampered lady tagging along on his summer explorations. But when his chance to join a prestigious expedition is on the line, he finds the ever-enthusiastic Miss Martin to be just the partner he needs.

Of Sea and Sorrow by Heloise C. Kensington

Disappointed in love, Edith Linton has given up on her dreams of matrimony and a home of her own. Concerned about her beloved brother's health, she acquiesces to a summer by the sea after her mother determines it is the only way to improve it, setting aside her own worries about her future.

Recently returned from the war in Crimea, Dr. Henry Forester hopes to improve medical practices in the seaside town of Weymouth, England. Not everyone is receptive to his new methods, especially his new patient's protective older sister.

Will Edith and Henry find a way to see past their differences? Or will all hope for the future pass before it has a chance to thrive?

Of Shells and Serendipity by Karen M. Edwards

Elspeth "Elsie" Abercrombie is a dutiful daughter—to a point. Although her mother tries to persuade her to marry, Elsie prefers to study marine biology. Dr. Magnus MacPherson, a former soldier, arrives to teach about battle wounds at the St. Andrews University Medical School for summer term. Magnus originally planned to return home to the Isle of Skye to establish a sanatorium until a sea change happens: a chance encounter with Miss Abercrombie and it's love at first sight. Can Elsie and Magnus reconcile their dreams and ambitions and find a love as deep and enduring as the constant sea?

Each book in the series is a standalone title. The stories may be enjoyed in any order.

www.ingramcontent.com/pod-product-compliance
Lightning Source LLC
Chambersburg PA
CBHW031517010826
48973CB00013B/2636